Reflection's Reckoning

The Mirror Kingdom: Book One

Amy N Kaplan

An imprint of Misfit Pages

Misfit Fantasy
Published by Misfit Pages
Texas USA

On the World Wide Web at www.misfitpages.com
First Published 2025

ISBN: 978-1-962613-25-5 (First Edition)

DEDICATION

For my children:

Jen, the chronicler of adventures.

Mary, whose spirit dances free as magic.

Chris, whose strength lies in compassion.

Josh W, whose ambition would make any realm prosper.

And Josh K, who finds laughter in the shadows.

You are my greatest story.

CHAPTER ONE: THE MIRROR'S CALL

Nadia's fingers trailed the spines of books on her shelf, each title a familiar friend beckoning her to distant lands and epic quests. Through her bedroom window, she could see the lake for which her town, Mirrorlake, was named; its surface so still it perfectly reflected the morning sky. She pulled out a novel, its edges worn from countless adventures within its pages. Sinking into her bed, she lost herself in the world of dragons and heroines, the silence of her room punctuated only by the occasional turn of a page.

The sun climbed higher, casting a warm glow through the window that danced across Nadia's features, highlighting the flecks of gold in her wavy auburn hair. Eventually, her mother's voice drifted up the stairs, gentle but persistent.

"Nadia, honey, let's go to the market. It'll be nice to get some fresh air."

With a sigh, Nadia marked her page and set the book aside. She joined her parents in their weekly ritual at Lakeside Park's farmers market, the social heart of Mirrorlake where the town's 12,000 residents gathered every Saturday. They wove through the bustling market filled with vibrant colors and the rich aroma of spices and fresh produce. Her parents chatted with vendors, picking out ripe fruits and fragrant herbs while Nadia trailed behind, her thoughts lingering on mystical creatures and hidden realms.

At home, Nadia helped prepare lunch, slicing vegetables with practiced ease while her father tended to a sizzling pan. The kitchen was alive with the symphony of cooking; the sizzle of onions in hot oil, the rhythmic chopping of knives against cutting boards, but even amidst this domestic harmony, Nadia's mind wandered to far-off battles and enchanted forests.

The afternoon unfolded with more weekend customs: board games Nadia played half-heartedly as she humored her parents' attempts at bonding; an old science fiction movie they'd watched together, its dated special effects prompting affectionate laughter; a family dinner where conversations meandered from mundane topics to her parents' recollections of their own youthful escapades.

Later that evening, Nadia met Jenny at their favorite hangout spot – an eclectic café adorned with local art and mismatched furniture. The buzz of conversation surrounded them as they settled into a cozy corner with two steaming cups of hot chocolate.

Jenny's eyes sparkled with excitement as she recounted the latest school gossip. "Did you hear about Mark and Lisa? They broke up!

Can you believe it?"

Nadia nodded along, offering appropriate reactions when needed. Yet even as she engaged in the banter, she felt a tug at her soul; a yearning for something beyond these teenage dramas.

As night enveloped Mirrorlake in its velvety embrace, Nadia walked Jenny home before making her own way back through quiet streets. She paused outside her house, gazing up at the stars peeking through the urban glow. Each one felt like a gateway to another world where magic was real and adventures awaited those brave enough to seek them out.

Inside her room once more, Nadia stared at her reflection in the mirror. A flicker of movement caught her attention. She spun around to look, but all she saw was the same pile of books waiting to be read on her floor. Turning to look in the mirror once more she thought she saw... something. Shaking her head wearily, she said aloud, "I must be tired. There can't be something else in here."

The weekend passed like countless others before it; comfortable yet tinged with an undercurrent of restlessness which no amount of normalcy could quell.

Sunlight filtered through the gauzy curtains of Nadia's bedroom, dust motes dancing like tiny fairies in the beams. She stretched beneath her covers, a groan escaping her lips as she reluctantly acknowledged the arrival of morning. The dreams of far-off lands and mystical creatures slowly faded, leaving a dull ache for adventure in their wake.

She rose, her wavy auburn hair a wild tangle around her shoulders. Padding across the room, she caught sight of herself in the mirror. Her bright green eyes stared back, hinting at the restless spirit lying beneath her calm exterior. Something flickered in the reflection, a shadow, a movement, something not quite right, but when she blinked and looked again, everything was normal. "I must not have slept well," Nadia muttered, running her fingers through her tangled hair. "I'm seeing things." With practiced motions, she tamed her hair into a semblance of order and chose her outfit for the day; a comfortable blend of jeans, her favorite dragon t-shirt and a soft hooded zip-up jacket which appeared to echo her desire for both familiarity and escape..

Descending the stairs to the kitchen, the comforting aroma of coffee and toasted bread enveloped her. Her parents were already there, moving in their well-rehearsed morning dance. Her father stood at the stove, expertly flipping pancakes; his Saturday ritual before heading to his accounting office above The Silver Needle. Her mother set the table, humming a tune from one of their favorite old sci-fi shows, a half-finished dress alteration draped over the nearby sewing machine.

"Morning, starshine," her mother greeted, her smile crinkling the corners of her eyes.

"Morning," Nadia replied, her voice still heavy with sleep as she slid into her usual seat at the table.

Her father turned from the stove, plate in hand. "I hope you're hungry," he said with a wink. "I may have gotten carried away."

The stack of pancakes before Nadia could have fed a small army. She laughed, carving off a portion and drenching it in syrup. "Thanks, Dad. I think I'll need all this energy to get through Mr. Kline's history test."

Her mother poured herself a cup of coffee and sat down opposite Nadia. "You've been studying all week," she said with confidence. "You'll ace it like you always do."

Nadia nodded but felt a twist in her stomach that had little to do with breakfast or impending tests. It was the same sense of longing for something more - something beyond quizzes and classrooms - that always appeared to simmer right beneath the surface.

As they ate, conversation flowed easily about mundane things: errands they needed to run, plans for an upcoming family movie night - comfortable chatter that wrapped around Nadia like a warm blanket. Yet even as she engaged and smiled, part of her mind wandered to distant realms where dragons soared and magic was as common as breathing.

"Earth to Nadia," her father teased as he caught her gaze drifting out the window to where morning light played upon leaves only beginning to hint at autumn's touch.

"Sorry," she said with a sheepish grin. "Just thinking about what book I should read next."

Her mother reached across the table, covering Nadia's hand with her own. "You always have your head in some story or another," she said with a fond smile. "Just make sure you come back to us now and then."

Nadia squeezed her mother's hand in response, grounding herself in the moment once more.

After breakfast was cleared away and goodbyes exchanged at the door, Nadia slung her Carrollton High backpack over one shoulder and stepped out into the crisp morning air. The familiar route to school awaited; another day among peers who never quite saw past the quiet girl who lived more in her head than out loud.

Yet as she walked along tree-lined streets with leaves crunching underfoot, Nadia couldn't shake off the feeling that somewhere beyond reflections and shadows, an adventure was waiting for her - an adventure that would soon turn all these ordinary days on their head.

Nadia spotted Jenny at their usual meeting spot, her laughter cutting through the crisp air like a bell. With Jenny, the walls Nadia built around herself melted away. She was the one person besides her parents who could pull Nadia out of her own head.

"Hey, weirdo!" Jenny called out, jogging over. "Ready for another thrilling day of watching paint dry?"

Nadia forced a smile. "As ready as I'll ever be."

Jenny's brows knitted together for a moment, catching the subtle undertone in Nadia's voice. "You okay? You've been kinda out of it lately."

Shrugging, Nadia glanced at the ground where shadows played tag. "Just tired, I guess."

Jenny linked arms with her friend, pulling her along. "Well, let me fill you in on the latest gossip to wake you up."

The duo walked side by side, Jenny chattering about who was dating who and which teacher had a meltdown during fifth period Friday. She paused mid-story to snap a photo of the autumn leaves overhead. "Perfect SnapLife aesthetic. Caption it 'another basic fall post' or 'living my best autumn life'?"

"Definitely the first one," Nadia said with a laugh. "More ironic."

At school, they navigated through throngs of students toward their lockers. The clang and bang of metal doors punctuated the air, mixing with snippets of conversation and bursts of laughter.

Jenny twirled the combination lock with practiced ease. "So, there's a party this Friday at Mark's place. You're coming, right?"

Before Nadia could answer, Jenny's phone was out and up. "Smile, bestie!"

"Jenny..." Nadia started to protest, but the camera click cut her off.

"And that's going on SnapLife," Jenny announced, already typing. "Day 147 of trying to get this hermit to a party."

Nadia rolled her eyes but couldn't help smiling. "I don't know yet about Friday."

"Come on," Jenny insisted, tucking her phone away. "You can't spend every Friday night with your nose in a book."

"I'll think about it," she conceded, managing a small smile at Jenny's familiar persistence.

Jenny sighed and closed her locker with a definitive snap. "You always say that."

They walked into homeroom together as the bell rang. The room settled into an uneasy quiet as attendance was taken and announcements droned on.

Nadia doodled in the margins of her notebook while Jenny passed notes with another friend across the aisle. Every now and then Jenny would shoot Nadia a sympathetic look or a silly face to make her smile.

As homeroom ended and students shuffled out toward their next class, Nadia lingered behind for a moment longer than necessary. She could feel Jenny's gaze on her back but couldn't muster the energy to explain this restless ache for something beyond these walls.

With a deep breath, she joined the flow of bodies moving through the hallways like currents in an endless sea.

Today was just another day... until it wasn't.

Nadia was there, but not quite present, her gaze adrift in the glow of the morning light. Around her, the symphony of high school life played on: the shuffling of papers, the tapping of pencils on desks, and the distant laughter trickling from the hallways. Nadia's English teacher, Mrs. Bell, droned on about reflections and duality in literature, her voice carrying an unusual intensity when discussing the darkness that lurked beyond the looking glass.

Nadia's pencil moved across her notebook, but not with notes from Mrs. Bell's lecture. Instead, she sketched creatures that leapt from the depths of her imagination onto the page; griffins with piercing eyes and dragons with scales shimmering like stars. Each stroke was an escape, a silent rebellion against the confines of the classroom walls.

A nudge from Jenny brought Nadia back to reality. Jenny arched an eyebrow and motioned towards Mrs. Bell who was now standing right beside Nadia's desk. "Miss Calder," she said, her eyes gleaming with something unreadable, "perhaps you'd like to share your... interpretations of Carroll's alternate world with the class?"

Heat rushed to Nadia's cheeks as she shook her head and mumbled an apology, tucking her hair behind her ear in a nervous gesture.

Mrs. Bell offered a half-smile that didn't quite reach her eyes before returning to her discussion about how Carroll's mirror world reflected the darkest corners of the human psyche. As she turned away, Nadia couldn't help but notice how the shadows appeared to cling to Mrs. Bell a moment longer than they should have.

The rest of English class passed in a blur for Nadia. When the bell finally rang, signaling the end of class, she felt a mixture of relief and frustration—relief she could put some distance between herself and her embarrassment, and frustration that she still felt trapped in this mundane cycle.

The hallways swelled with students as Nadia made her way to history class. She found herself squeezed between athletes boasting about last night's game and clusters of students huddled over smartphones. In history class, Mr. Kline had planned a test on ancient civilizations - a subject Nadia usually found fascinating.

Today, however, as Mr. Kline handed out the test papers, Nadia couldn't help but feel disconnected from it all. She wrote her name at the top of the page and looked down at the first question:

"In what ways did geography impact the development of Mesopotamian civilization?"

Nadia bit her lip and glanced around the room; everyone appeared absorbed in their work - everyone but her. She sighed softly and turned back to her test, willing herself to focus.

She answered each question methodically but without her usual passion for history. The minutes ticked by like hours until finally, Mr. Kline called time.

Nadia handed in her test without looking Mr. Kline in the eye and slipped out of class with a whisper-thin sense of accomplishment - if only because it was over.

Gym class awaited next - a stark contrast to sitting still and filling out scantrons.

The gymnasium smelled like polished wood and echoed with the sound of squeaking sneakers. Coach Martinez had them running laps today. As Nadia's feet found their rhythm on the gleaming floor, her mind began to wander. The circular track became a winding path through an ancient forest, the fluorescent lights above transformed into dappled sunlight filtering through silver leaves.

"Nadia! Keep it up!" Coach Martinez's voice snapped her back to the harsh gym lights and the steady thud of running shoes.

She picked up speed automatically, focusing on the simple rhythm of her feet against the floor. By the time class ended, Nadia was breathless, her daydreams forgotten in the simple exhaustion of physical exercise.

Late morning edged toward noon as Nadia moved through hallways lined with lockers reflecting flashes of students passing by like fish in a stream.

The hallway was a blur of activity - posters for upcoming dances, gleaming sports trophies in their cases, clusters of students planning their weekends. Nadia moved through it all like a ghost, distracted by a strange feeling she couldn't shake. Something was different about today, though she couldn't say what.

The final bell rang, signaling the end of fourth period and the start of lunch. Students spilled into the hallways, a cacophony of chatter and the shuffle of feet on linoleum echoing off the lockers. Nadia joined the flow, her thoughts drifting to the odd occurrence earlier that morning.

She caught up with Jenny at their usual meeting spot by the cafeteria entrance. Jenny was animatedly discussing weekend plans with a group that parted as Nadia approached.

"Hey, you spaced out big time in English today," Jenny said, nudging Nadia playfully. "Dreaming about your knight in shining armor or bored out of your mind?"

Nadia managed a smile. "Just tired. But hey - weird thing. This morning my reflection... it like, moved wrong? By itself?"

Jenny's eyes widened for a split second before she laughed. "Girl, you definitely need more sleep. Or maybe less fantasy novels. They're starting to mess with your head!"

They grabbed their trays and found a table by the window. Jenny immediately arranged her lunch with practiced precision.

"Seriously?" Nadia raised an eyebrow. "You're SnapLifing your cafeteria pizza?"

"Content is content," Jenny replied with a solemn look before breaking out into a grin. "Besides, I'm going for a 'school lunch reality check' series."

The lunch period passed with Jenny regaling tales of her cousin's latest escapades, and before they knew it, the bell was ringing again.

When the bell rang again, they dumped their trays and joined the crowd heading back to class. The afternoon started with study hall, where the silence was broken only by the occasional page turn and the soft buzz of Jenny's phone. Nadia glanced over to see her friend scrolling through her SnapLife feed.

"Look," Jenny whispered, tilting her screen. "Someone caught Mr. Peterson dancing in his classroom when he thought everyone had left."

Nadia bit back a laugh as Mrs. Harris, the study hall monitor, shot them a warning look.

The period dragged until finally the bell sent them to science class, where Mr. Parker announced they'd be dissecting frogs.

"Oh my god, no," Jenny said, clutching Nadia's arm. "I can't. I literally can't. It's still looking at me." She shuddered and hid behind Nadia as their specimen lay on the dissection tray.

"It's not looking at anything anymore," Nadia said, trying not to laugh as Jenny peeked over her shoulder. "Here, I'll make the first cut if you'll take notes."

"You're my hero," Jenny declared, placing her hand over her heart with a dramatic flair. "But I'm still not touching it. What if it jumps?"

"Jenny, it's definitely not jumping anywhere."

In homeroom, they sat through schoolwide announcements - upcoming dances, sports events, and reminders about report card dates. Nadia doodled absently in her notebook margins, adding wings to her latest creature sketch while the announcements droned on.

Finally, the last bell echoed through the halls. Books slammed shut, chairs scraped against floors, and students burst forth into the freedom of post-school hours.

Nadia and Jenny walked side by side toward home, their steps in sync from years of taking this same route together. Jenny was still going on about Mark's party.

"You're coming with me this time," Jenny insisted. "No excuses!"

"I already said I'll think about it," Nadia replied with a non-committal shrug.

They reached Nadia's house first. She fished her keys from her backpack as Jenny continued to outline potential outfits for them both.

"See you tomorrow," Nadia said as she unlocked the door.

"Text me later!" Jenny called out as she walked backward down the path, phone already up. "And check your SnapLife - I'm posting the best shot from that disaster of a frog dissection!"

Nadia stepped over the threshold into her home's familiar embrace. Silence welcomed her; a stark contrast to the day's constant buzz. She dropped her backpack by the door and exhaled deeply.

This was where she could unravel her thoughts without distraction. This was where another world was eager to whisper its secrets through mundane reflections.

The absence of her parents' presence echoed off the walls, their daily routine pulling them elsewhere. A folded piece of paper, weighted down by the ceramic salt shaker, caught her eye on the kitchen counter. Her mother's cursive looped across the page; a list of chores to complete before dinner.

She skimmed through the tasks: vacuuming the living room, dusting the bookshelves, watering the indoor plants. A sigh escaped her lips. She tossed her backpack onto a chair and grabbed the dust cloth from its drawer.

As she wiped away invisible particles from the polished wood of the bookshelves, Nadia's eyes flicked to the hallway mirror. She paused, leaned closer. Her reflection mimicked her movements with perfect synchrony. For a moment, she searched her own eyes for the odd flicker of movement she thought she'd seen earlier in the day, but nothing appeared amiss. With a shrug, she turned back to her task.

She moved through her chores with efficiency, though not without frequent glances at her reflection in any surface that could give one. The glass door of the microwave revealed a girl with auburn waves tied back into a loose ponytail; the black screen of the television showed her silhouette framed by stacks of DVDs.

Each mirror encounter was like a magnet drawing her in, an invisible thread pulling at her curiosity. The dining room's ornate mirror framed her face as she fluffed cushions on the chairs; nothing unusual there either.

As she watered ferns and philodendrons, Nadia's phone buzzed. Three new SnapLife notifications from Jenny, probably documenting her walk home with her usual running commentary. Nadia ignored them for now, her attention drawn once again to her reflection in the small hand mirror on the windowsill. A beam of sunlight lanced through it, creating rainbows on her skin. She twisted it in her hands, watching colors dance across her face but found no other magic at play.

The chores neared completion; all that remained was her bedroom; the final frontier for today's mundane mission. She climbed the stairs with light steps, still pondering the strange occurrence from earlier

Nadia's room greeted her with its comforting clutter: posters of distant galaxies and mythical landscapes plastered on walls, piles of books teetering on her nightstand. And there it stood in its usual corner; the weathered wooden mirror that appeared to harbor more tales than all her books combined.

She approached it slowly, heart thumping with a mix of anticipation and trepidation. Nadia stared into its glassy depths, waiting. Her reflection gazed back with equal intensity - a silent

challenge hanging between them.

Nadia's heart thrummed in her chest like a bird desperate to escape its cage. The mirror, with its age-old secrets and intricate carvings, had always been an object of fascination for her, but today it beckon her with an urgency she couldn't explain. Her hand, almost of its own volition, reached out towards the glass that had shimmered with a strange light just moments ago.

With a tentative touch, she expected the cool, hard surface of her reflection. Instead, her fingers met no resistance; they slipped through the mirror as if it were liquid, sending ripples across the glass. A gasp caught in her throat and she recoiled, yanking her hand back as if burned. It emerged unscathed but trembling.

"This isn't possible," she whispered to the empty room.

But the mirror stood silent, its secrets still veiled behind an inviting glow.

The urge to call Jenny was immediate. She fumbled for her phone, fingers still tingling from the encounter with the impossible.

"Jenny, you've got to come over," Nadia blurted out when her friend answered.

"What's up? You sound like you've seen a ghost."

"It's... I can't explain it over the phone. Please, just come."

Skepticism laced Jenny's voice. "Is this about the reflection thing at lunch?"

"Just hurry," Nadia urged.

A click signaled Jenny's reluctant agreement before the line went dead.

Left to her own devices and with curiosity gnawing at her reason, Nadia glanced around her room for something – anything - to test the mirror's limits. Her gaze landed on a paperback fantasy novel splayed open on her bed. She picked it up and approached the mirror once more.

Hesitation shivered down her spine as she held the book towards the glassy surface. With a nudge, she pushed it forward and watched in awe as half of it disappeared into the mirror. Pulling it back revealed no changes; it was as if the book had never breached another realm.

"This is insane," she murmured to herself.

Next came a stuffed animal - a worn bear with one eye missing and fur matted from years of love and adventure. Nadia pressed its paw against the mirror and again it slipped through without resistance.

"Teddy's halfway to another world," she joked weakly to herself.

She tried other items: a pencil that appeared to write invisible letters on an unseen page when half-submerged in the mirror, a hairbrush which appeared to be grooming an invisible doppelganger's hair on the other side, even a flickering candle that didn't extinguish when half of it was engulfed by the glass.

Every item returned unaltered after its partial journey into the unknown - a fact that both disappointed and relieved Nadia. It meant there were rules to this magic; it wasn't complete chaos. But what did it mean for living things? She couldn't help but wonder if her hand had come back unchanged...?

Almost as an afterthought, Nadia pulled out her phone. Jenny would never believe this without proof. She snapped a quick SnapLife of her pencil halfway through the mirror's surface, then another of her teddy bear's paw disappearing into the glass. But when she checked the photos, they showed only normal reflections - as if the mirror was merely a mirror after all.

A glance at her clock by the bed told Nadia that Jenny would arrive soon. She took a deep breath and leaned closer to the mirror. Her reflection did too, mirroring each movement with perfect synchrony except for the one moment earlier when....

"Maybe I imagined it," Nadia mused aloud, trying to shake off the eerie feeling clinging to her skin like morning dew.

But deep down, she knew she hadn't imagined any of it. The mystery was real and waiting on the other side of that ordinary-looking glass.

Nadia steeled herself for Jenny's arrival and what might come next because once she shared this secret, everything would change. There was no going back from a truth so fantastical that reality itself would bend in its presence.

Nadia's heart raced as she gazed at the mirror, her reflection an insistent beacon urging her forward. Her hand trembled, hovering over the surface that had swallowed her touch moments before. Jenny's delayed arrival gnawed at her resolve, but the lure of adventure whispered louder than the pull of patience.

With a deep breath, she stepped through. The world shifted. Cool air caressed her skin, scented with wildflowers and an undertone of something ancient and indefinable. Nadia blinked against an unexpected brilliance, her eyes adjusting to a landscape that was basically pulled straight from her beloved fantasy novels.

She fumbled for her phone, hands shaking with excitement. Jenny had to see this. But her attempts to capture the silver-leafed trees and violet blooms on SnapLife showed only a black screen. Her texts wouldn't send, and her heart sank as 'No Service' mocked her from the screen. Her thumb hovered uselessly over the keyboard; there was no way to tell Jenny where she was or what she'd found.

The world before her unfurled like a living tapestry. Massive trees stretched toward an opalescent sky, their silver leaves tinkling in a gentle breeze like wind chimes made of starlight. Their melody harmonized with the distant calls of unseen creatures, creating a symphony unlike anything in her world. She stood on a pathway bordered by violet blooms, their petals delicate and otherworldly against the emerald backdrop. Ahead, mountains pierced the sky with obsidian tips, shrouded in mist lending an air of mystery to their grandeur. Below, rivers wove through valleys like threads of quicksilver, pooling into lakes shimmering beneath an ever-shifting sky.

Nadia's eyes roamed across the beautiful vista, wonder eclipsing fear. Each breath felt like drinking from a cup of pure enchantment. Yet as she turned back to ensure her lifeline remained intact, a knot formed in her stomach - the portal was but a mirror hanging in open air, reflecting a slice of her own room.

The sound of a door opening echoed from somewhere beyond

the mirror.

Back in Nadia's world, Jenny let herself into the house with the spare key she'd been entrusted for emergencies just like this. "Nadia?" Her voice bounced through the quiet rooms, each echo feeding her growing concern. "This better not be another one of your dramatic reading sessions where you've got your headphones on and can't hear anything!".

The house was undisturbed; a chore list lay half-completed on the kitchen counter, bearing silent testament to Nadia's presence mere moments ago. Jenny ascended the stairs two at a time and pushed open Nadia's bedroom door.

Sunset bled through the windowpane, spilling over the old mirror in the corner. She approached it cautiously; this was where Nadia had sounded most excited and most afraid.

Jenny's reflection stared back at her from within its aged frame - a perfect mimicry save for one chilling detail: it wasn't hers alone. Beyond her shoulder, Jenny could see another figure in the glass – Nadia - her back turned and walking away into an impossible distance filled with colors and light no earthly place could hold.

Jenny reached out to touch Nadia's vanishing image but met only cold glass; no passage opened for her as it had for her friend. She pressed harder, desperation mounting when her hand refused to break through the barrier between worlds.

"Nadia!" Her voice cracked against the silence of the room, unanswered by anything other than her own reflection's troubled gaze.

CHAPTER TWO: A WORLD UNVEILED

In the heart of the strange forest, Nadia stood alone, her breath visible in the crisp air. The canopy above her twisted into elaborate patterns, filtering sunlight into a mosaic of shimmering gold and emerald hues. Trees unlike any she had ever seen rose from the ground, their bark glistening with a sheen of silver and their leaves a vibrant shade of lavender fluttering in a gentle breeze.

With each step, the forest floor cushioned her feet with a layer of moss so thick and soft it felt like walking on clouds. The air hummed with the quiet whisper of life hidden out of sight. Leaves rustled, twigs snapped under the careful tread of unseen creatures, and the scent of flowers and earth mingled in her nostrils.

Nadia's gaze followed the flitting shadows dancing just beyond her periphery. In one moment, she caught sight of a creature resembling a rabbit, but with antlers spiraling like delicate vines reaching for the sky. Its eyes sparkled with an intelligence that suggested awareness of her presence, yet it bounded away without fear.

A bird called out from above, its melody harmonizing with the whispering trees. It had feathers that transitioned from deep blue to vibrant purple, leaving traces of color as it soared through beams of light. The forest responded to its song; branches swayed and leaves trembled as if they too were part of the chorus.

Further along, Nadia stumbled upon a brook babbling with laughter as it wound its way through the forest. She knelt beside it, dipping her fingers into its crystal-clear waters that tingled with vitality. The water tasted sweet on her lips - refreshing in a way tap water never could be.

Curiosity pulled Nadia deeper into the woods, each step revealing more wonders. Flowers unfurled at her approach, petals iridescent and glowing faintly in the dim light beneath the trees. Some blossoms had shapes that defied logic; spirals felt like they went on forever and blooms that opened only to reveal another flower within.

As Nadia wandered, she came upon a clearing where light cascaded down like a spotlight on nature's own stage. Here she saw creatures that looked like butterflies but were as large as hawks. Their wings shimmered with an array of colors so vivid they could only be plucked from dreams. They fluttered around her briefly before ascending towards the canopy.

She pressed on, finding herself amidst trees bearing fruit in every imaginable color - and some beyond imagination. They hung heavy on branches arching toward her as if offering their bounty. With cautious reverence, Nadia plucked a fruit shaped like a star with skin as smooth as silk and shades blending from yellow to deep red at its tips. She bit into it tentatively; it burst with flavor - both sweet and tangy - and juice dribbled down her chin.

Intrigued by every rustle and chirp, Nadia tried to spot more inhabitants of this strange place. A family of bushy-tailed creatures scampered along tree branches overhead; their chatter filled the air as they leaped from limb to limb with acrobatic grace.

The forest felt alive in a way Nadia couldn't explain - a pulse throbbing beneath its serene exterior. There was no sign of human or humanoid life; instead, this world was inhabited by beings both familiar and fantastical.

Nadia found herself standing before a tree unlike any other - a giant whose trunk spiraled upwards into infinity. Its leaves pulsed softly with light from within as if containing a heartbeat of their own. From its branches hung chimes made from an unknown crystal-like material that sang with the wind - a symphony that touched something deep within her soul.

It was here in this clearing, surrounded by chimes' music and bathed in dappled sunlight, that Nadia felt an odd sense of belonging - an anchor in this foreign land where she had been swept away by curiosity and wonder.

She took out her phone once more, not expecting service but

feeling compelled to document this moment somehow. Swiping open the camera app, she snapped photos of the glowing leaves and twisted silver bark, then a quick video of the chimes as they sang their ethereal song in the breeze. The images appeared on her screen but looked flat and washed out - dull shadows of the vibrant reality surrounding her.

Frustrated, Nadia tried typing notes instead: "Trees with silver leaves. Air smells like cinnamon and rain. Flowers glowed from within." Words felt inadequate, like trying to describe a symphony with stick figure drawings.

She opened SnapLife out of habit, finger hovering over the "New Story" button before she caught herself. No service meant no posting, and somehow it felt right. This place wasn't meant to be filtered and shared. It was meant to be experienced.

As she lowered the phone, what caught her attention was her reflection in the darkened screen - a girl out of place yet perfectly at home among these marvels. She pocketed her device, deciding some memories were better kept in the heart than in pixels.

Movement caught Nadia's eye - a delicate fae-like creature hovering near one of the glowing leaves. It was no larger than her thumb with wings so transparent they could have been made from spun glass. It regarded Nadia for a moment before flitting away towards the upper reaches of the spiral tree.

The deeper into this strange new world Nadia ventured, the more she realized how little she knew about this place and how much there was to discover. Each creature she encountered was another mystery to unravel; each plant another enigma beckoning to be understood.

Although she could not name these beings or speak their language - if indeed they had one - she felt an inexplicable kinship with them all: fellow inhabitants of a universe vast beyond comprehension yet intimately connected by threads unseen.

With every breath she took amid these wonders - each inhalation tasting like life itself - Nadia's heart swelled with newfound courage and determination. This realm may have been unknown to her mere hours ago, but now it called to something deep within her - a call she couldn't ignore or deny.

A gentle breeze caressed her face then - as if acknowledging her silent pledge - and Nadia smiled back at it before stepping forward once more into this new world's embrace.

Nadia's heart raced as she navigated the ethereal forest, each step an echo in a symphony of rustling leaves and distant bird calls. The towering trees, with their silver leaves chiming like delicate bells, cast dappled shadows on the ground and played tricks on her eyes. She had never seen anything like the spectacle before her - each breath she drew tasted of magic and wildflowers.

Suddenly, the quiet harmony of nature's music gave way to the sound of approaching footsteps. Nadia stilled, her fingers tightening around her phone. She watched as two figures emerged from between the trees, their forms shimmering at the edges as if bathed in the dappled sunlight filtering through the canopy.

The taller one, with a stride matching the calm of the forest, had short auburn hair that caught the glint of the ever-changing sky. His piercing green eyes met hers, and for a moment, Nadia felt as though she were looking into a familiar reflection, though she couldn't place why. There was something in the set of his jaw, in the way he carried himself, it stirred a strange sense of recognition.

The other figure was older, his weathered face etched with lines that spoke of wisdom earned through years of vigilance. His silver-streaked hair was pulled back in a practical style, and the cloak draped across his broad shoulders seemed to shift between green and brown with each movement, blending with the forest around them. His presence commanded attention - not through intimidation but through a quiet strength radiating from him like heat from embers. When he spoke, his voice was a deep timbre that resonated with the wisdom of ages.

"Who are you?" Nadia asked, her voice betraying none of the apprehension knotting in her stomach.

"I am what you see in your own reflection," replied the young man with an air of solemnity. "My name is Aidan."

The older figure bowed slightly; his gaze unwavering. "I am Garin," he said.

Nadia took a cautious step back, her mind racing to make sense of what she was seeing. "How can you be my reflection? And where am I?"

"You stand in Mirrathia," Garin explained, "a realm that exists beyond your world."

"Mirrathia..." The name rolled off Nadia's tongue like a forgotten dream trying to surface. Her pulse quickened as she considered the implications.

"Yes," Garin added with a nod. "You have crossed through the portal between our worlds."

Aidan stepped closer, his expression earnest. "Some connections transcend worlds," he said, answering her first question with deliberate vagueness. "Your arrival here is no accident."

Questions swirled in Nadia's head like leaves caught in an autumn gale. Why her? What did they expect from her in this strange land? She glanced at her phone - the screen remained stubbornly void of signal bars.

"What do you want from me?" Nadia asked, trying to keep her voice steady.

Aidan exchanged a glance with Garin before responding. "It is not just what we want; it is about what you are prophesized to do here."

Garin stepped forward then, his eyes reflecting an ancient sorrow. "We have long awaited your arrival," he murmured. "Mirrathia is in peril."

Nadia swallowed hard; this was more than any fantasy novel plotline - it was real and happening to her.

"And how am I supposed to help with that?" she asked, skepticism edging into her voice despite the otherworldly scene around her.

Aidan's gaze locked with Nadia's, an intensity in his eyes drawing her in. The woods around them whispered secrets, the leaves rustling with an ancient rhythm as if in conversation with the wind.

"You're not here by chance," Aidan began, his voice a calm stream flowing over the uncertainty churning within Nadia. "Mirrathia is bound to you, and you to it. You wield a power innate and profound - control over light."

Nadia blinked, processing his words. The notion of possessing power was foreign, fantastical. She folded her arms across her chest, a protective gesture against the swelling tide of revelation.

"Control over light?" she echoed. "What does that even mean?"

Aidan glanced skyward where sunlight filtered through the towering trees, casting a mosaic of light and shadow on the forest floor.

"It means," he continued, "that within you lies the potential to harness the very essence of illumination. To push back darkness, to reveal truth hidden in shadow."

Nadia's eyes widened as Aidan extended his hand toward a beam of sunlight. The light coalesced around his fingers, bending and brightening until it formed a radiant orb hovering above his palm.

"Queen Bellinor" he said, his voice dropping to a whisper as the orb dimmed and dissipated into the air, "fears this power."

Nadia felt her heart pound in her chest like a drumbeat echoing through the forest. She could sense an energy within her, a dormant force awaiting a spark.

"Queen Bellinor," she said, tasting the name on her tongue.

Aidan nodded gravely.

"She is cloaking this land in perpetual twilight to strengthen her reign." He gestured toward the horizon where darkness pressed against the fading light. "Her dominion grows each day, fed by shadows and fear."

Nadia turned away from Aidan, looking deep into the forest where shapes moved in obscurity - perhaps normal creatures or perhaps something more sinister. The thought sent a shiver down her spine.

"How can I... How can anyone stand against such power?" she asked.

Aidan stepped closer, his presence reassuring.

"Because light is potent - a beacon in darkness. And because you are not alone." His voice held a promise that pierced through Nadia's doubts like rays of sunshine through cloud cover.

Nadia mulled over his words. A part of her wanted to dismiss them as fantasy - impossible tales spun by her imagination fueled by too many books and movies. But another part resonated with an unexplainable truth as if something deep within had awakened at Aidan's call.

Garin watched from a distance, his expression unreadable yet tinged with anticipation.

"What am I supposed to do?" Nadia finally asked, her voice barely above a whisper.

"Learn," Aidan replied, shrugging. "Train your abilities, understand your connection to Mirrathia."

"And then?"

"And then," he said with determination lighting his features, "you shine."

As if on cue, the sun broke through a gap in the canopy overhead and bathed them in golden warmth; a stark contrast to the encroaching gloom threatening from afar.

The air was charged with an electric current when Nadia glanced at her own hands, as ordinary as ever, and wondered if they could indeed wield such incredible power. Could she be this beacon Aidan spoke of? The thought was both exhilarating and terrifying.

Nadia started to back away toward where she'd entered this realm. "I should go back. This is all too..."

"Before you decide," Aidan interrupted, his tone gentle, "there's something you should see."

Before Nadia could respond, a chilling screech echoed through the forest. The shadows beneath the trees began to writhe unnaturally, coalescing into shapes with gleaming eyes. "Shadow Trackers," Garin hissed, drawing a sword from beneath his cloak. "They've found the portal." Aidan grabbed Nadia's arm. "We must leave now. If they capture you..." "But the portal..." "Will lead them straight to your world," Aidan finished. "Is that what you want?" Nadia's blood ran cold at the thought of those writhing shadows following her home to her parents, to Jenny.

"No, I..." Nadia stammered, her mind reeling with images of shadow creatures in her parents' living room, stalking Jenny through school hallways.

"Good, let's go then!" Aidan said, turning toward the deeper forest.

Nadia cast one last glance at where the portal had been, then followed the two strangers into the unknown, praying she'd made the right choice.

CHAPTER THREE: MOON HOLLOW

The forest became a blur of silver leaves and shadow as they ran. Nadia's lungs burned, her legs aching as she struggled to keep pace with Aidan and Garin. Behind them, the chittering screech of the Shadow Trackers grew fainter but never completely disappeared.

"This way," Garin hissed, veering left onto what looked like no path at all.

Nadia trailed behind Garin, each step taking her deeper into the realm's heart. The trees whispered secrets in a language she could not understand, their leaves rustling with the knowledge of ages. The air was fragrant with the scent of flowers unseen, their perfume a tapestry woven from threads of vanilla and wild jasmine.

"Who are the Shadow Trackers?" Nadia asked.

"The Shadow Trackers are stealthy spies and assassins. They

blend into shadows and use poisons and mind manipulation to gather intelligence for Bellinor," said Aidan.

"You two need to keep your voices down or they'll hear us," warned Garin.

The forest gave way to undulating hills that rolled like waves toward distant mountains. Here, creatures of light and shadow frolicked amidst the tall grasses - luminescent butterflies flitted through the air, their wings like shards of stained glass, while tiny, furred beings darted between Nadia's feet, chittering in playful tones.

Garin led silently, his eyes scanning the horizon with a vigilance born from years of guardianship. His hand rested on the hilt of an ancient blade, its presence a silent oath to protect.

"How does he even know where we're going?" Nadia gasped when they finally slowed to a walk.

Aidan glanced at Garin before answering. "Garin and his wife, Talia, raised me," he said simply. "He's been teaching me to navigate Mirrathia since I was young enough to hold a practice sword."

As they ascended a rise carpeted with wildflowers, Nadia caught sight of the mountains that loomed like sentinels guarding the horizon. Their peaks pierced the sky with such majesty that she felt her breath catch in her throat.

"These mountains have stood since time immemorial," Aidan said, his voice tinged with reverence. "They've witnessed the rise and fall of kingdoms and have weathered storms born from the deepest sorrows."

Nadia marveled at their grandeur, feeling an echo of their

timeless strength within her own bones.

They reached a chasm where mist curled around towering spires like serpents made of smoke. A narrow bridge spanned the gap, its arc crafted from vines that intertwined with an elegance that belied their strength.

Garin lead the way, his steps measured and sure as they crossed into an area veiled in silver fog. The air was cool and damp against Nadia's skin, carrying whispers of secrets yet untold.

Emerging from the mist, they found themselves on a precipice overlooking a vast expanse where shadows danced at the edge of vision. Nadia peered into the depths below, where valleys lay shrouded in twilight's embrace.

Aidan stood beside her, "Below lies our destination, Moon Hollow," he said, voice low.

Nadia strained her eyes to see more clearly but found only glimpses of structures hidden among the folds of darkness.

Garin's voice broke through her concentration. "We must still tread carefully," he warned. "Allies abound, but so do traitors."

The descent was steep and treacherous; loose stones skittered down inclines at missteps while shadows stretched long fingers toward them as if to snatch them away from safety.

They'd barely gone twenty paces when Garin held up a hand. A soft whistle echoed through the darkness - three short notes followed by one long. Garin responded with a similar pattern, and suddenly two figures materialized from behind nearby boulders, bows drawn.

"Garin? Is that you?" one of the sentries asked, lowering his weapon slightly.

"Aye, Marten. With Aidan and... a guest."

The sentries exchanged glances, their arrows still notched. "No one mentioned new arrivals tonight."

"It was unplanned," Aidan interjected. "The Shadow Trackers found our portal. We had to move quickly."

After a tense moment, the guards lowered their bows. "Pass, then. But Captain Grey will want to hear about this immediately."

As they continued their descent, Nadia noticed more sentries positioned along the path, some visible, others betrayed only by the slightest rustle of movement. The rebels clearly took their security seriously.

They halted at last on an outcrop overlooking the outpost; a collection of huts and tents nestled against a protective ring of boulders. Campfires dotted the encampment like terrestrial stars; figures moved about them with purposeful strides.

Aidan placed a hand on Nadia's shoulder. "This is our refuge," he said. "Here we gather strength for what lies ahead."

Garin surveyed their surroundings one final time before nodding his assent - a silent declaration that for tonight, at least, they had reached sanctuary's edge without incident.

Together they stood as twilight deepened around them - three souls bound by fate on the cusp of rebellion's haven.

Garin's figure receded into the depths of a large tent, the fabric flap falling behind him with a silent weight that echoed the gravity of their situation. Aidan turned to Nadia, his green eyes reflecting the flickering campfires as he offered her a reassuring nod.

"This is Moon Hollow," he said, gesturing to the lively encampment around them. "The heart of our resistance."

Nadia took in the panorama of rebellion life unfolding before her. Her gaze followed the tendrils of smoke rising from campfires to where they mingled with the evening sky. The air carried a mélange of sounds - metal clanging in rhythmic harmony from the blacksmith's corner, laughter and soft chatter emanating from clusters of rebels sharing stories of narrow escapes and daring raids.

Aidan led her past a group practicing swordplay, their movements fluid and precise, an intricate dance Nadia could only watch in awe.

"These are some of our finest warriors," Aidan said, as one landed a deft strike on her opponent's wooden sword. "They've all sworn to protect Mirrathia from Bellinor's shadow."

A young man with braids falling over his shoulders paused mid-swing, offering a nod in Nadia's direction before resuming his training.

As they continued, Aidan introduced her to the denizens of Moon Hollow. There were beings she had only encountered in her books: a healer, Clara, with hands that glowed with a soft light as she tended to a wounded soldier; scholars debating over ancient texts and scrolls; a tinkerer whose table was strewn with gadgets and crystals.

One figure caught Nadia's attention - a woman weaving light itself into what appeared to be a shield. She worked with an effortless grace, strands of luminance bending at her will.

"They call her Lysara," Aidan whispered. "She has mastered the art of lightweaving."

Nadia watched, mesmerized as Lysara finished her work and gave them a knowing smile before turning back to her craft.

Further into Moon Hollow, they approached a table laden with maps and models representing various terrains and strongholds.

"These are our strategists," Aidan explained. "They plan our defenses and assaults."

Nadia peered at the maps, trying to make sense of the various markers and symbols that were foreign to her eyes.

"We must always be ten steps ahead," said one strategist without looking up from his discussion.

They moved on, each introduction and encounter building upon Nadia's understanding of this world that was both hers and not hers.

"You'll find we're more than just fighters here," Aidan said as they came upon a circle of musicians filling the air with an uplifting melody. "We keep our culture alive through music, art... it reminds us what we're fighting for."

A girl about Nadia's age played a stringed instrument with fervor, each note ringing out like a call to arms against despair.

At last, they arrived at a mix of tents and wooden structures that provided shelter and comfort for those recently arrived or displaced by Bellinor's forces.

"This is where you'll stay until you find your footing in Mirrathia," Aidan told her. "You'll be safe here among friends."

Nadia nodded, though her mind was still racing with all she had seen - the camaraderie, determination, and sense of purpose that infused every aspect of life in Moon Hollow.

Aidan appeared to read her thoughts. "It's overwhelming at first," he admitted. "But you'll grow into it. This place has a way of bringing out the best in us."

He paused then, as if considering his next words carefully. "And you... you have so much potential, Nadia."

Her cheeks warmed under his gaze; she felt exposed yet strangely fortified by his confidence in her.

Just then, a commotion near the entrance caught their attention - a group was returning from an expedition beyond Moon Hollow's protective boulders. Their faces were etched with fatigue but alight with triumph. Among them was Garin who strode forward with purposeful steps toward Aidan and Nadia.

His expression softened as he approached them, his warrior facade giving way to that of the mentor he had always been for Aidan... and now for Nadia too.

"We have much to discuss," Garin said quietly but firmly. His eyes met Nadia's for an instant before he turned back toward the leaders' tent at the rear of Moon Hollow.

Aidan nodded once more at Garin's retreating form before turning back to Nadia with an encouraging smile.

"Come on," he said gently. "Let's find you something warm to eat. You must be starving after all this excitement."

And together they walked back into the heart of Moon Hollow where rebels shared their meals as freely as they shared their dreams for Mirrathia's future free from darkness.

The low hum of conversation and the clinking of cutlery against earthenware bowls filled the dining tent. Lanterns hung from the canvas ceiling, casting a warm glow on the rebel faces gathered around the long wooden tables. Nadia, her senses alight with the scents of spiced stew and fresh bread, felt a strange mix of excitement and unease.

Aidan guided her to a seat beside a woman whose serene countenance belied the scars that traced her arms. Her eyes, soft and knowing, met Nadia's with a welcome that needed no words.

"This is Clara," Aidan introduced, "our healer."

Clara's hand enclosed Nadia's in a gentle grasp. "You're safe here," she assured her, voice as soothing as the melody of a distant flute.

Across from Nadia sat a man whose presence she thought could command the air itself. Lines etched his weathered face like battle maps, each scar a tale of defiance. His hair was peppered with gray, but his eyes held an unwavering sharpness.

"And this is Captain Grey," Aidan said. "He leads us."

Captain Grey nodded curtly at Nadia, appraising her with an intensity that made her want to look away, but she held his gaze.

"We're glad you've found your way to us," he said. His voice was gravelly, as if each word were carved from stone.

Nadia managed to smile before turning her attention to the meal before her. The stew was hearty, filled with root vegetables and chunks of meat that fell apart at the touch of her spoon.

As they ate, Clara and Captain Grey spoke in turns, painting a picture of Mirrathia's plight under Bellinor's shadowy grip.

"Bellinor seized power years ago," Clara began, stirring her stew absentmindedly. "She was once part of the Royal Council but hungered for more than just a seat at the table."

"Her ambition led her to dark magic," Captain Grey cut in. "She found ancient texts that spoke of shadow weaving; an art long forbidden for its corrupting touch."

Nadia listened intently, absorbing every word as if it were a lifeline that could help her navigate this strange new world.

"With shadow weaving," Clara continued, "Bellinor could bend darkness to her will. She staged a coup, extinguishing any light that opposed her."

"The Shadow Keepers are her enforcers," Captain Grey added with a scowl. "Taskmasters rule through fear; Shadow Trackers silence any whispers of dissent; Shadow Priests twist faith into fanaticism; and her Shadowguard... they are the worst of them all."

Nadia set down her spoon, "The Shadow Trackers. They were the ones that followed us from the portal."

Captain Grey's chair scraped against the floor as he shot to his feet. "What? You were followed?" His face darkened as he rounded on Garin. "You didn't mention Shadow Trackers!"

Garin, who had been quietly eating at the far end of the table, looked up sharply. "We lost them in the forest. I didn't think..."

"You didn't think?" Captain Grey's voice rose. "If even one made it past our outer sentries..." He was already moving toward the tent flap, barking orders to nearby guards. "Double the watch! Send scouts to backtrack their path!"

Clara placed a calming hand on Nadia's arm as the captain's commands echoed through the camp. "Don't worry," she murmured. "Grey takes our security very seriously. If any Shadow Trackers were still following, our sentries would have found them."

Despite Clara's reassurance, Nadia couldn't shake the guilt settling in her stomach. Her arrival had already brought danger to these people who had offered her sanctuary.

After a moment of tense silence, Clara cleared her throat softly. "Well, we've spent all this time talking about us," she said, her warm smile returning. "Why don't you tell us a little about you? We're all quite curious about the girl who stepped through a portal."

Before Nadia could respond, her body betrayed her with a massive yawn. The events of the day - stepping through a mirror, fleeing from Shadow Trackers, discovering this hidden rebel camp - suddenly crashed over her like a wave.

Clara chuckled softly. "Or perhaps that conversation can wait until morning. You've had quite the day."

"I'll show her to the guest quarters," Aidan offered, rising from the table.

The 'guest quarters' turned out to be a small but comfortable tent near the edge of the camp. A simple cot with wool blankets awaited her, along with a basin of water and a small oil lamp.

"Try to get some rest," Aidan said, pausing at the tent flap. "You're safe here."

But sleep didn't come easily. Nadia lay awake, her mind racing with questions. Had the Shadow Trackers found her home? Was Jenny safe? Her parents? And why did everyone here look at her with such expectation, as if she held some key to their salvation?

The occasional footsteps of sentries passing by her tent only heightened her anxiety. Each sound made her wonder if the Shadow Trackers had somehow found them.

Eventually, exhaustion won out, and she drifted into a fitful sleep filled with shadows and whispers.

Morning came too soon, announced by the sounds of the camp stirring to life. Nadia emerged from her tent to find Aidan waiting with a bowl of porridge and dried fruit.

"Breakfast?" he offered with a smile that suggested he too hadn't slept well.

They made their way to the communal eating area where Clara and several other rebels were already gathered. Captain Grey was notably absent - likely still coordinating security measures.

Clara waved them over. "Good morning! I hope you managed some sleep despite everything."

As Nadia settled onto a bench, Clara picked up their conversation from the night before. "Now then, you were going to tell us about yourself?"

Nadia took a spoonful of porridge, buying herself a moment. "There's really not much to tell. I'm just... ordinary."

"No one who steps through a portal is ordinary," Clara said.

The conversation soon turned back to the rebellion, and Nadia found herself asking the questions that had kept her awake.

"The people suffer," Clara murmured. "But we resist." Her gaze shifted to Nadia. "We fight for those who cannot."

"How?" The question slipped from Nadia's lips before she could catch it.

Garin leaned forward. "We strike where we can - supply lines, outposts... We free those we can from labor camps." He paused as if considering his next words carefully. "But Bellinor's strength lies in darkness. To truly defeat her, we must bring back light."

Nadia felt all eyes on her then, an unspoken expectation hanging heavy in the air.

Aidan reached over and placed his hand atop hers in silent support.

"You speak of light as if it's... tangible," Nadia said slowly.

"It is," Clara replied with conviction. "Just as darkness fuels Bellinor's power, light will be our salvation."

Nadia thought about what Aidan had told her yesterday about her dormant abilities - could she really be key to bringing light back to this place?

Nadia's fingers lingered on the rough grain of the wooden table, tracing the carvings etched into its surface. The flickering flames of the nearby fire danced in her eyes, casting shadows across her face. Captain Grey's words hung heavy in the air, laden with sorrow and resolve.

"We've lost much to Bellinor's reign," he said, his voice a low rumble like distant thunder. "Families torn apart, children orphaned... our land suffocates under her shadow."

Clara nodded, her gaze never leaving Nadia. "We fight not for glory, Nadia, but for a chance at a future where our children can play beneath the sun without fear."

Nadia's heart clenched at their words. Her own world felt like a distant memory, one where her biggest concern had been an unyielding history test and the strange behavior of her reflection. Here, in Mirrathia, reality bore the weight of oppression and conflict.

"I... I understand your struggle," Nadia murmured, her voice barely above a whisper. "But I'm not a warrior and I can't use magic. I'm a girl who found herself here by accident."

Aidan leaned forward, his eyes earnest. "But you're not here by accident, Nadia. Mirrathia called to you for a reason."

Nadia shook her head fiercely. "I need to go back. My parents will be worried sick. My friend Jenny... she's probably scared out of her mind. What if the Shadow Trackers went through the portal?"

Silence enveloped them as they regarded the young girl who was so out of place among the seasoned faces of rebellion.

Clara reached out and placed a gentle hand on Nadia's shoulder. "Your compassion is clear, as is your longing for home." Her voice softened. "Perhaps when you return to your world, you'll carry our stories with you."

Nadia met Clara's eyes and saw not only hope but an unspoken plea.

Nadia's eyes flitted between Aidan and Clara, and then to Captain Grey's stoic face. She bit her lip, caught between worlds and responsibilities that were probably too vast for her shoulders.

As they exited the tent into Moon Hollow's morning air, Nadia shivered slightly against the dawn chill. The sky above was transitioning from deep indigo to soft pink, the last stars fading as the sun began its climb. The camp was coming alive around them - the sounds of clanking cookware and quiet conversations replacing the night's silence.

The rebels moved about the outpost with quiet efficiency, their faces etched with lines of determination and fatigue. Some tended to weapons while others repaired armor or prepared food for those returning from scouting missions.

Nadia watched as a young boy no older than herself sharpened his sword with meticulous care. His eyes held none of the joy or mischief one might expect from someone his age - only focus and something akin to resignation.

She approached him tentatively.

"Hey," she said.

He glanced up at her briefly before returning his attention to his blade.

"You're about my age," Nadia observed aloud.

He nodded without looking up again.

"Do you ever wish... you could be doing normal kid stuff? Not fighting in some war?"

Finally, he met her gaze fully. "Every day," he admitted. "But this is our reality now." He paused before adding quietly, "What about you?"

Nadia swallowed hard as their eyes locked; an understanding passing between them without words.

In that moment, something shifted within her, growing kinship with these people who had been thrust into turmoil through no choice of their own.

As day dawned around Moon Hollow and whispers of plans and strategies filled the air like an undercurrent to the crackling fires, Nadia sat beside Aidan once more.

"I can't pretend I'm not scared," she confided to him as they watched the rebels move like shadows against the flames.

Aidan offered a small smile that didn't quite reach his eyes. "Fear is natural," he said. "It reminds us we're alive."

"And if I help," Nadia said, tentative. "What then? How do I know it will make a difference?"

"You don't," Aidan replied. "But sometimes we must act without assurance of success - because it's right."

They sat together in silence as Nadia mulled over his words and considered what part she might play in this unfamiliar narrative woven with threads of courage and despair.

Eventually, Aidan stood up and extended his hand to help her rise from where she sat on the ground. His gaze held hers firmly yet gently as he spoke again.

"Whatever choice you make, Nadia," he said. "Know that it is yours alone."

With that statement hanging in the air like mist on the morning grasses of Mirrathia's fields, they walked back toward where Garin had disappeared earlier into his tent; a silent sentinel awaiting their return.

In the light of the rebel outpost's central tent, a map sprawled across a large table. The rebels' murmurs rose and fell like the ebb and flow of a distant tide. Captain Grey leaned over the map, his fingers tracing paths through forests and mountains, his scars casting shadows that mimicked the craggy terrain.

Nadia stood at the edge of the gathering, her eyes flitting from face to face, absorbing the resolve etched into each one. The scent of pine and woodsmoke from the morning fires mingled with the lingering taste of porridge on her tongue.

Aidan sidled up beside her, his presence a strange comfort in this unfamiliar place. "You look like you've seen a ghost," he whispered, his brow creasing in concern.

She shook her head, trying to dislodge the unease that settled there. "Just trying to understand all this," she admitted.

Captain Grey's voice cut through their whispers as he straightened up, addressing the room. "We're not merely fighting for land or freedom. This is about survival." His gaze landed on Nadia, and for a moment, silence enveloped them like a cloak.

"Nadia," he began, his voice a low rumble. "Your arrival here isn't mere chance."

She stiffened, feeling every eye in the tent on her now. "What do you mean?"

He walked over to her, his steps measured and deliberate. The other rebels parted to let him pass. "There's an ancient prophecy among our people," he said as he stopped before her. His voice carried weight like stones in deep water.

Aidan frowned, glancing between Nadia and Captain Grey. He had heard whispers of prophecies but never lent them much credence.

Captain Grey continued, "It speaks of one 'born thrice,' first in flesh then in reflection." His gaze flickered to Aidan then back to Nadia. "And finally born anew when their true power awakens."

Nadia felt Aidan tense beside her as they both considered the words. It was too close to their own strange tale not to feel a prickle of destiny brushing against their skin.

"And this one," Captain Grey said with measured emphasis, "will draw forth a 'blade of stars' to banish darkness from our land."

Silence reigned as Nadia processed his words. Her mind raced with images of light forging weapons and darkness retreating before them.

Under the pale morning sky, Nadia sat across from Aidan, their bowls empty from the simple breakfast shared with the rebels. Moon Hollow's morning fires sent thin wisps of smoke curling upward, and the camp was alive with quiet activity. The dawn air carried the fresh scent of dew-covered grass and the soft chirping of birds greeting the new day.

"So, Nadia, you've stepped through a mirror into a world unknown," Aidan began, his voice laced with curiosity. "But what of your own origins? What tales lie within your family history?"

Nadia shifted uncomfortably, the bench beneath her suddenly feeling harder than it had moments ago. She gazed into the flames, her mind reaching back through years of memories.

"I know little about my lineage," she admitted, tucking a loose strand of hair behind her ear. "My parents never spoke much of their past. I never met my grandparents, and cousins are strangers to me."

Aidan leaned forward, resting his elbows on his knees. "But surely there must be some trace of your heritage. A name, a place?"

She shook her head. "We've always lived in Mirrorlake. It's quaint and quiet; barely a blip on the map. They moved there when I was an infant."

The silence between them stretched like a thin veil, delicate and revealing. Aidan pondered this simplicity, contrasting it with the complexity that had been his own life in Mirrathia.

"And your mirror," he prodded gently, "the one that served as your gateway to this realm... Does it hold significance in your family?"

Nadia's eyes flickered with remembrance. "It's old, an heirloom passed down through generations. I've always felt drawn to it, though I can't explain why."

Aidan nodded thoughtfully. His own memories stirred... the mirror in his room, the glimpses of a girl who looked startlingly familiar yet impossibly distant. "I had a mirror too," he said. "In my room at the cottage where Garin and Talia raised me. Sometimes I'd see you there - reading, drawing, living your life in that other world."

Nadia's eyes widened. "You could see me?"

"Not always. Just... moments. Flashes." He smiled ruefully. "Talia helped me understand it was a connection to another realm, though she never explained why I could see you specifically." He paused, studying her face. "I used to wonder if you could see me too."

Nadia shook her head slowly. "No, I... I only saw myself. Until yesterday, when everything changed."

The sun rose as they conversed; stories unfolded from Nadia like petals opening at dawn. Tales of her childhood adventures in her backyard, of her parents' kindness and their simple life filled with books and movies.

Aidan listened intently, finding himself drawn to the contrast between their worlds - hers so grounded in reality yet touched by an undercurrent of something extraordinary; his, a tapestry woven with light and shadow.

The outpost buzzed with an undercurrent of tension. Rebels huddled in small clusters, their voices low, faces etched with worry and determination. Moon Hollow, once a haven of whispered strategy and hopeful rebellion, now bristled with the sharpening of blades and the tightening of bowstrings.

Nadia lingered at the edge of the gathered crowd; her mind awhirl with the recent torrent of revelations. She watched as Aidan, a mirror image yet so distinctly otherworldly, wove between the rebels, his presence reassuring yet commanding.

The flaps of a tent whisked open, drawing all eyes. A scout, cloaked in shadow-worn leathers, emerged into the sunlight. Murmurs ceased; breaths held.

"The Shadow Keepers," the scout announced, his voice cutting through the silence like a cold draft. "They muster forces not four day's march from here."

A collective shiver ran through the assembly as if winter had whispered its chill into their bones.

Captain Grey stepped forward, his brow furrowed. "Numbers? Which faction?"

"Shadowguard leads," replied the scout, "backed by Taskmasters corralling prisoners to fortify their camp."

Clara's fist clenched at her side. "They mean to crush us before we can gather strength."

Captain Grey's eyes narrowed; his voice was steel wrapped in velvet. "We must decide our course swiftly. Do we fortify and prepare for siege or strike first against this encroachment?"

Voices rose like a sudden gale, each rebel pitching their strategy into the growing storm of debate.

Nadia felt Aidan's gaze upon her and turned to meet it. His eyes searched hers as if looking for an anchor in this tempest of fear and resolve.

"We cannot let fear dictate our actions," Aidan addressed the crowd. "We strike with precision; we strike as one."

The Dawnguards nodded, murmurs of agreement rising among

them.

Garin reappeared at that moment, his expression unreadable. He moved through the crowd and whispered something into Captain Grey's ear.

The captain's eyes flickered with an unreadable emotion before he addressed the assembly once more.

"Prepare yourselves," he commanded.

The crowd dispersed to ready themselves for battle while Nadia remained still, her thoughts racing like leaves caught in a whirlwind.

Aidan approached her then, his face somber yet resolute. "You don't have to fight," he said.

"I know," Nadia replied. "But I can't stand by either."

They stood side by side for a moment that stretched long and thin like a silver thread about to snap.

"You've got spirit," Clara said as she joined them, her smile wry but warm. "I can see why the prophecy might speak of you."

Garin cleared his throat sharply, shooting Clara a warning look.

Clara's eyes widened slightly as she caught herself. "That is," she amended quickly, "you have the courage we value in all our fighters."

Nadia nodded silently but inside she felt anything but true; still an outsider looking in on a world she barely understood.

The sun rose higher in the sky, spreading its warmth across the camp as plans were drawn and preparations made. The very air was charged with anticipation and dread; a prelude to the clash that awaited them.

Nadia found herself alongside Captain Grey as he surveyed maps scattered across a table strewn with markers and figures.

"Where do I fit into all this?" Nadia asked quietly.

Grey peered at her over the rim of his glasses, a gesture oddly reminiscent of teachers back home, and then down at the maps before him.

"Your place is here for now," he replied. "Safe within Moon Hollow's bounds."

"But..."

"No buts," he interjected, his tone firm but not unkind. "You've no training for what comes next."

Nadia bit back her protest and nodded reluctantly.

Silence fell over Moon Hollow like snowflakes on an abandoned field, soft yet cold, beautiful yet foreboding.

Rebels clad in dark attire slipped through the trees like shadows given form; a stark contrast to Nadia's own brightly colored school clothes that screamed 'outsider' among this sea of camouflage and purpose.

Garin approached her then, his gaze holding depths untold as he offered her a simple dagger; the handle worn from use yet sturdy in its make.

"For protection," he said, before turning to join Aidan at the forefront of their gathered force.

Nadia weighed the dagger in her hand, its presence both comforting and terrifying, and slipped it into her belt loop where it hung hidden yet accessible beneath her hoodie.

Whispers of strategy became currents flowing through the crowd as they made ready... a murmuring river poised to break free from its banks and flood the world with change.

Nadia, absorbed in her own thoughts, jolted at the sound of a low whistle. Aidan stood a few feet from her, the morning breeze tousling his short auburn hair.

"Come on," Aidan called, a smile playing on his lips. "We've got work to do."

Nadia asked. "What do you mean?"

"Time for you to learn control," he said with an earnestness that brooked no argument.

She followed him out into the clearing, dew from the grass soaking through her boots. The crisp air filled her lungs and nudged away the last vestiges of doubt. Aidan led her to a secluded spot where the warm rays of the sun filtered through the canopy above.

"Now," Aidan began, his tone shifting to one of instruction, "focus on your core. Lightweaving is about balance and harmony."

Nadia closed her eyes, trying to envision some inner light or energy as Aidan described. She concentrated until her head throbbed but felt nothing resembling power or light.

"I don't think it's working," Nadia admitted, opening her eyes to find Aidan's patient gaze.

"Give it time," he encouraged. "Envision the light emanating from within."

She closed her eyes again, this time reaching deeper into herself, searching for a flicker, a spark, anything. Minutes stretched on as she strained for a sign of her abilities.

Aidan watched Nadia struggle with her first attempt at lightweaving, her frustration evident in the crease of her brow. The scene stirred something in him, a memory of his own first lessons with Garin in a moonlit glade years ago.

"Patience," he said softly. "None of us mastered it quickly."

Nadia's eyes met his, questioning. "How long did it take you to learn?"

Aidan's hand absently touched the hilt of his practice sword; the same one Garin had given him on his first day of training. "Years," he admitted. "And I'm still learning."

As he spoke, memories washed over him...

Garin, with his weathered face and eyes that had seen the turning of centuries, watched over Aidan like a sentinel from the past. The old guardian had become father, mentor, and protector ever since the fateful day when Aidan's parents succumbed to a darkness that had crept into Mirrathia like a silent plague.

"You must be swift as the wind," Garin instructed as they stood in the heart of the glade. His voice was firm but carried a gentle undercurrent. "Your movements should leave no trace."

Aidan nodded, focusing on the stance Garin had taught him. He balanced on the balls of his feet, his body coiled and ready. The air around them practically hummed with anticipation.

Garin lunged forward with a practice sword, its blade catching the waning light. Aidan parried with an agility that belied his young age, his counterstrike nearly catching Garin off guard.

"Good," Garin praised with a nod. "But never let your guard down."

The sparring continued until stars began to prick through the veil of dusk. It was then that Aidan's true potential began to unfurl like a nocturnal bloom.

With every sweep of their wooden swords, an unusual shimmer traced Aidan's movements; a subtle glow that neither boy nor guardian could ignore. It flickered like a flame caught in a breeze but did not extinguish.

"Aidan," Garin said, lowering his sword as he studied the boy's outline etched in light. "You have begun to weave."

Aidan's heart skipped a beat at those words. Lightweaving was an ancient art in Mirrathia, one both revered and feared for its power and potential for ruin.

"Is it dangerous?" Aidan asked, though part of him already knew the answer.

"It can be," Garin replied. "It requires control and understanding."

In secret, they honed this newfound ability. Garin's wife Talia, who possessed lightweaving skills herself, took on the role of instructor during those clandestine sessions.

"Feel the light within you," she would say as they sat under moonlit skies. "It is part of you, as much as your breath or your blood."

Aidan learned to shape beams into lattices and orbs into barriers, light became his canvas; his will, the brush.

Yet there were moments when darkness appeared to seep from him involuntarily; times when shadows gathered at his fingertips more readily than light. In those instances, Talia looked upon him not with fear but with a solemn kind of wonder.

"You have a rare gift," she said one evening as shadows danced around them like curious specters.

Aidan remembered feeling a thrill at her words mingled with an edge of trepidation. His shadow weaving was powerful—more so than his lightweaving, and instinctively he knew it held dangers he could not yet comprehend.

"We must keep this between us," Talia urged him with an urgency that tightened her voice. "If others were to know..."

Aidan nodded solemnly; he understood what lay at stake—their safety, their very lives in Mirrathia could hang in the balance if word spread of his dual nature.

The years passed; seasons cycled from bloom to barrenness and back again. Aidan grew taller, leaner—a mirror image of resilience sculpted by Garin's tutelage and tempered by secrets harbored in silence.

They practiced in hidden glens and shadowed groves; Garin never ceased pushing Aidan toward mastery over both light and dark. Yet even as Aidan's skills flourished under their watchful eyes, so too did the whispers of unrest beyond their secluded life.

"It is time you learned more about your heritage," Garin announced one morning after their training session had ended with Aidan executing a flawless sequence of lightweaves.

Aidan straightened up from where he knelt on the ground, catching his breath after their rigorous practice.

"My heritage?" He wiped sweat from his brow as curiosity lit up his features.

"Yes." Garin took a seat on an ancient stump worn smooth by time and weather. "You were born into this world amidst prophecy and strife."

The air grew still around them, as if nature itself leaned in to listen to Garin's tale; a tale woven from threads of love, loss, and destiny.

"Your parents were great leaders," Garin said, while Aidan listened intently to every word about figures he couldn't remember but felt connected to by blood and fate alike. "They knew you were special; destined for greatness or... perhaps calamity."

Garin paused then stood up abruptly; it was clear there was more he wished to say but couldn't or wouldn't divulge just yet.

"We will speak more on this later," he decided after a moment heavy with unspoken truths hanging between them like ripe fruit too perilous to pluck from its branch.

Aidan nodded silently; questions burned within him, but he knew better than to press for answers when Garin wore such an inscrutable expression.

That evening as stars blinked overhead casting their cold light upon Mirrathia's undulating landscape, Aidan sat alone by a reflective pool deep within their hidden sanctuary; a sanctuary threatened by forces unseen yet palpable as if woven from nightmares spun into reality by some malevolent loom...

In the cool, dusky hours of twilight, when shadows grew long and the world softened into hues of lavender and grey, young Aidan had often found himself drawn to the glade beyond the thickets of Mirrathia. It was there, beneath the boughs of whispering trees, that his story with Garin began; a story entwined with secrets and the discovery of his own latent powers.

The memory faded as Nadia's voice brought him back to the present.

"It's like trying to grab smoke," she said with exasperation.

Aidan's lips pressed into a thin line. "Sometimes it's not about grasping but letting go."

Nadia mulled over his words but found no solace in them. Her hands clenched into fists at her sides.

"I just feel... normal," she confessed, voice tinged with defeat.

Aidan placed a reassuring hand on her shoulder. "You are far from normal, Nadia. Your power will come in time."

As they stood there in silence punctuated only by distant murmurs of camp activity, footsteps approached through the underbrush. Garin emerged into the clearing with someone in tow; a woman with wise eyes and hair like spun silver.

"Nadia Calder," Garin announced in his gravelly voice, "this is my wife, Talia."

The woman stepped forward with grace that belied her years. "I'm here to help you find your way," she said.

Her presence seemed to carry an unspoken promise: where Aidan and Nadia had met frustration, she would usher in understanding and growth.

Aidan exchanged glances with Garin; both knew that if anyone could awaken Nadia's abilities, it would be Talia.

CHAPTER FOUR: A POWER AWAKENED

Three days had passed since Garin had introduced Nadia to his wife, Talia. Morning draped Moon Hollow in a tapestry of golden light and dew-kissed cobwebs. The rebel outpost stirred to life, the gentle clatter of breakfast mingling with the rustle of leaves. Nadia watched the sun peek through the trees, feeling a sense of peace, she hadn't known she'd been missing.

Garin emerged from his tent, his eyes reflecting a solemnity that matched the gravity of their situation. He gestured for Nadia to follow him. She trailed behind, her steps hesitant, until they reached a clearing where Talia awaited them, her gaze as piercing as it was kind.

"Nadia," Talia began, her voice as smooth as a serene lake. "Awakening your powers is akin to remembering a language you once spoke fluently but have since forgotten. It's there, in your spirit, waiting for your call."

Talia extended her hand and a soft glow emanated from her palm. The light pulsed as if it was alive, an ethereal dance that hypnotized Nadia. "Let your instincts guide you. Reach out to the light within."

Nadia closed her eyes and took a deep breath. She felt the warmth of the morning sun on her face and imagined reaching inward to a hidden part of herself. She extended her hand but felt nothing more than the morning chill nipping at her fingers.

Clara joined them, placing a gentle hand on Nadia's shoulder. "Patience," she whispered, her presence a balm to Nadia's budding frustration. "The journey is as important as the destination."

They spent hours under Talia's tutelage, coaxing Nadia's powers with whispered encouragements and shared visions of light. But as shadows lengthened and morning turned to afternoon, Nadia's powers remained stubbornly dormant.

Lysara arrived as the afternoon waned, her silver-blue eyes holding depths untold. She brought with her an air of quiet determination that filled Nadia with renewed hope.

Over the next week, Nadia's training intensified. Each morning began with Talia, trying to coax her dormant abilities to life. Afternoons were spent with Lysara, learning the theory behind lightweaving even if she couldn't yet practice it.

"Lightweaving is an art," Lysara explained while unraveling strands of light from the air itself. They swirled around her like living sculptures, mesmerizing in their complexity. "You must feel each thread as an extension of your own essence."

Nadia watched in awe as Lysara manipulated the light into forms both beautiful and functional, a shield here, a sword there, all glowing with an inner luminescence.

"Try to feel the light as you would the warmth of a blanket or the caress of a breeze," Lysara said.

Nadia focused again, reaching out with senses she didn't know how to use. By the end of the first week, Nadia had managed only the faintest glimmer at her fingertips a spark that faded as quickly as it appeared.

Clara took a different approach in the second week. "Sometimes," she said, leading Nadia to a quiet glade, "we try too hard to force what should flow naturally."

She rolled up her sleeve, revealing a small cut on her forearm. "Watch closely." Clara placed her other hand over the wound, and a gentle golden light emanated from her palm. The skin knitted together before Nadia's eyes, leaving no trace of injury.

"Healing light comes from compassion," Clara explained. "It's gentler than the light used for protection or battle. Try thinking of someone you love who needs help."

"Your turn," Clara said, using a small knife to make another shallow cut on her arm.

Nadia thought of Jenny, of her parents, of the fear she'd felt when the Shadow Trackers had pursued them. She placed her hand over

Clara's wound, focusing on her desire to help. A tiny spark flickered in her palm, steadier this time, though still weak. The cut began to close, though not as quickly or completely as when Clara had demonstrated.

"Good start," Clara encouraged. "Healing takes practice and patience."

"Strength comes not only from knowing oneself but also from understanding one's place in the world," Talia added, having watched the lesson. "You have seen our struggle here, let it fuel your desire to learn."

The sun dipped below the horizon as they continued their attempts. Shadows played across Talia's face while she watched Nadia grapple with invisible forces only she could touch, if only she could figure out how.

"You're pushing too hard," Clara said. "Sometimes power awakens not through force but through acceptance."

Nadia nodded but couldn't hide the disappointment etched into her features, the furrowed brow, the downcast eyes.

They decided to try one last time before sleep beckoned them all into its embrace. Talia stepped forward once more.

"Close your eyes," she instructed. "Envision your energy intertwining with that of Mirrathia, the land itself."

Nadia complied, taking slow breaths as she pictured roots extending from her feet into the earth beneath her, a network connecting her core to that of Mirrathia.

There was a flicker within her, a warmth that spread from heart to limb, and when she opened her eyes again, they were met by gasps from those around her.

Her hands glowed with an inner fire—the first whisper of dawn after an endless night, and within those flames danced threads of incandescent light that wove around her fingers like strands of fate entwining.

A smile tugged at Lysara's lips while Clara's eyes brimmed with tears unshed, tears not of sorrow but of joy for this first step on what would be a long journey ahead.

Lysara approached Nadia slowly and spoke words laden with pride and hope: "This is only the beginning."

Nadia's fingers trembled as she focused on the tiny orb floating before her, its luminescence flickering like the last ember of a dying fire. The surrounding forest of Moon Hollow hushed as if in anticipation, leaves rustling in soft whispers. Lysara, with her silvery hair cascading over her shoulders, stood close, watching with an encouraging smile.

"Let it grow from within," Lysara advised, her voice a melodic hum that resonated with the rhythm of the woods.

Nadia's brow furrowed, the weight of expectation heavy on her shoulders. She exhaled slowly, trying to channel the sense of wonder she felt as a child when she first discovered fireflies dancing in the dusk of her backyard. The orb pulsed, responding to her thoughts, its light waxing for a heartbeat before waning once more.

Aidan observed from a distance, his green eyes reflecting the struggle mirrored in his reflection's effort. He knew patience was a tree whose roots took time to entrench before it could bear fruit.

Clara joined Lysara's side, arms crossed. "She has the spark," Clara noted. "But sustaining it? That's where true control lies."

Talia approached; her expression unreadable. "Control is not just mastery over power; it's mastery over self," she said, her gaze locked on Nadia.

As the minutes stretched into what felt like hours under the watchful eyes of her mentors and newfound friends, Nadia's arm lowered in defeat. The orb dissipated into a wisp of light that vanished into the evening air. She let out a sigh that carried her frustration into the treetops.

"I can't keep it lit," she admitted, shoulders slumping.

Lysara stepped forward and placed a gentle hand on Nadia's shoulder. "You're too hard on yourself. Lightweaving is an art that takes time to perfect."

"I don't have time," Nadia countered, shaking off Lysara's touch. "Every moment I fail is another moment Bellinor strengthens her hold."

"You're not failing," Aidan interjected as he approached. "You're learning."

Nadia met Aidan's gaze, searching for a shred of doubt in his confident demeanor but found none. His assurance was a sturdy bridge over her uncertainty.

"It feels like failing," she confessed, kicking at a stray pebble with her boot.

Aidan chuckled softly and picked up a fallen leaf from the

ground. "Do you think this leaf failed when it let go of its branch?"

Nadia considered the question before shaking her head.

"It simply followed its nature," Aidan continued, twirling the leaf between his fingers before letting it glide to the ground. "Your nature is not to force light into existence but to let it flow through you."

"But how can I let it flow if I can't even feel where it starts?" Nadia asked.

Aidan stepped closer and lowered his voice to a fraction above a whisper. "It starts where everything begins... with a single thought, a single desire."

"Desire for what?" Nadia's question hung between them like mist.

"To protect? To heal? To illuminate darkness?" Aidan offered possibilities like stars waiting for Nadia to connect them into constellations.

"I want... I want to understand why I'm here," Nadia breathed out, voicing a longing that had nestled within since stepping through the mirror portal.

"Understanding will come," Aidan reassured her. "But first, you must trust yourself as much as we trust you."

Nadia closed her eyes and drew in a deep breath, trying to untangle her thoughts and focus on that trust... trust in herself and trust in this peculiar destiny that had chosen her.

"Try again," Aidan encouraged gently.

With renewed determination and Aidan's belief fueling her spirit like kindling to flame, Nadia extended her hand once more. This time she imagined warmth spreading from her heart through her veins to her fingertips where another orb slowly began to take shape... a testament not only to light but also to perseverance.

The orb wavered but held steady longer than before; its glow gentle yet unyielding as if borrowing strength from Nadia's resolve. Her mentors shared a look of quiet approval, and Aidan let a small smile slip through, one that spoke of hope and hard-won progress... not perfection.

A sense of accomplishment flickered within Nadia but was quickly doused by an errant thought... a memory of Jenny's puzzled expression back home, which caused the orb to flicker out once again.

"The day will come when your thoughts won't disrupt your focus but enhance it," Aidan said as if reading her mind.

Nadia gave him a wry smile. "Until then?"

"Until then," Aidan echoed with warmth lighting up his features, "you'll have us by your side."

And so they stood together in Moon Hollow as twilight embraced them, a young girl who had stepped through a mirror into destiny and a young boy who had lived in its reflection all along—each finding solace in shared resilience under an ever-watchful sky.

As the second week progressed, Nadia's control improved incrementally. She could maintain a small orb of light for several seconds before it flickered out. Her frustration remained, but hope had taken root.

Aidan watched Nadia, her eyes alight with the same restless curiosity that had driven her through the mirror. Her gaze lingered on the vibrant canopy above, where light played hide and seek with shadow. Despite his caution, he understood her yearning; Mirrathia, after all, was a realm of wonders.

"We must tread carefully," he reminded her. "The woods are not just beauty and light. Dangers lurk where you least expect them."

Nadia nodded but the glint of adventure in her eyes remained undimmed. "I just want to see everything," she confessed.

Lysara approached, her presence a serene counterpoint to Nadia's bubbling enthusiasm. "There is wisdom in the desire to explore," she said. "But also wisdom in heeding caution."

With a gentle smile, Lysara beckoned Nadia. "Walk with me. The woods hold lessons for those willing to learn."

They ventured into the forest, a tapestry of silver leaves rustling a song of ancient times. Lysara moved with an elegance that borrowed from the very air of Mirrathia itself, each step a silent communion with the earth beneath her feet.

"The light within you is more than a tool or weapon," Lysara began as they walked along a path lined with towering trees. "It is your guide, your protector, and your companion."

Nadia listened intently, her earlier frustration with her training dissipating like mist under the morning sun.

"Mirrathia responds to those who respect its balance," Lysara said. "Trust in your light, and it will reveal paths unseen by eyes clouded with doubt or fear."

The forest seemed to listen, a gentle breeze weaving through the branches as if nodding in agreement.

"How do I trust something I can't control?" Nadia's voice was soft but earnest.

"Control is an illusion," Lysara said, stopping to touch the trunk of an ancient tree. "True mastery comes in understanding and partnership. Work with your light, not against it."

A silvery leaf drifted down from above, landing in Nadia's open palm, a sign of acceptance from Mirrathia itself.

They came upon a clearing where sunlight danced across the ground in playful patterns. Lysara raised her hand, and strands of light gathered around her fingers like silk spun from morning dew.

"Watch," she instructed as she wove the light into a shimmering orb that floated above her palm.

Nadia's eyes widened at the display, her heart thrumming with excitement.

"The first step is to see your light as part of you—a reflection of your innermost self." Lysara's voice was calm yet carried an undercurrent of potent energy.

Nadia mirrored Lysara's gesture tentatively. Her fingertips quivered slightly as faint wisps of light began to gather before her.

"Good," Lysara encouraged. "Now let it grow naturally, do not force it."

The orb flickered uncertainly before stabilizing into a soft glow that warmed Nadia's face.

"It's beautiful," she said, wonder lacing her words.

Lysara smiled. "And it is yours, unique as your spirit."

As they continued their walk, Lysara shared tales of Lightweavers past, heroes who had shaped Mirrathia's destiny not by force but by understanding their gifts' true nature.

"Your abilities are more than mere manipulation of energy," Lysara explained as they navigated through thickets brimming with fragrant blossoms. "They are an expression of harmony between you and this world."

Nadia considered this, feeling an intrinsic pull towards something greater than herself, a connection to Mirrathia that transcended mere physical presence.

"But what if I fail?" Doubt crept into Nadia's voice like an unwelcome shadow.

Lysara stopped and placed a hand on Nadia's shoulder. "Failure is merely another step on the path to wisdom. Each falter teaches us more about our strengths, and our resolve."

A glimmer caught Nadia's attention, a flower unfurling its petals as if awakened by their conversation.

"And when darkness threatens?" she asked.

"The strongest light shines brightest against the dark," Lysara replied without hesitation. "Trust that yours will do so when needed."

Their path took them deeper into Mirrathia's heart, where secrets whispered from every leaf and stone, a symphony of life that embraced them both.

As they emerged from the woods' embrace into Moon Hollow once more, Aidan waited anxiously. He could see the change in Nadia, subtle yet undeniable, the way she held herself spoke of newfound confidence mingled with humility.

Lysara offered him a knowing glance before departing with a graceful nod.

"You've been gone for hours," Aidan said, relief coloring his tone.

Nadia smiled—a reflection not only of joy but understanding too. "I've learned so much."

He could tell there was truth in her words; there was a different radiance about her now, an inner light that found its echo in Mirrathia's glow around them.

"And?" Aidan prompted curiously as they walked back towards the encampment together.

Nadia glanced at him, a twinkle in her eye reminiscent of starlight piercing through night's veil, and simply said:

"I'm ready to learn more."

Clara led Nadia to the lake, a tranquil body of water reflecting the sky's shifting palette, as dusk began to unfurl its cool embrace. The gentle healer moved with a grace that smoothed the very air they passed through. They settled on the grassy bank, where the sounds of the forest wove a hushed lullaby, punctuated by the occasional splash of fish leaping for their evening meal.

"Close your eyes, Nadia," Clara murmured. "Breathe in the life around you, breathe out your doubts and fears."

Nadia obeyed, her chest rising and falling in rhythm with Clara's instructions. She could feel the damp earth beneath her, grounding her presence in Mirrathia. With each breath, the weight of her uncertainty began to shed, drifting away like leaves on the water's surface.

"Now," Clara continued, "envision a spark within you, as small and as potent as a seed waiting to burst forth into bloom."

Nadia concentrated, her brow furrowing as she imagined a tiny point of light in her core. It was faint at first, an elusive glimmer that danced barely beyond her mental grasp.

"Do not chase it," Clara said. "Let it come to you."

Nadia adjusted her approach, relaxing her mind's eye, allowing space for the light to grow. And there it was, a soft glow between her hands that she hadn't noticed before. She held them apart tentatively, fearing any sudden move might snuff out the fledgling brightness.

"Excellent," Clara breathed out in encouragement. "Now let it grow."

With Clara's guidance and her own burgeoning will, Nadia coaxed the light wider, feeling its warmth tickle her palms. It was like nurturing a sunrise within her hands, small flickers of light slowly but confidently expanding.

The corners of Nadia's lips turned upward in a silent smile of triumph. Her heartbeat synced with the pulse of light between her palms; it was both a part of her and something entirely otherworldly.

The meditation continued with Clara's voice a steady beacon in the growing evening. The stars above began their nightly vigil, casting down silver glances upon the pair by the lake. In that moment, Nadia felt an ember of belief kindling within, belief in Mirrathia's magic and in herself.

The small flickers grew bolder under Nadia's command, now less like shy fireflies and more akin to steadfast flames. They wove around each other in an intimate dance choreographed by an unseen force, a testament to Nadia's awakening power.

Clara sat back on her heels and watched as Nadia shaped the light into forms only limited by imagination: here a bird taking flight, there a flower blooming at unnatural speed. Each creation was ephemeral but filled with radiant life before dissolving back into mere potential.

The confidence that infused Nadia's movements became tangible; it flowed from her like a river freed from winter's grip. Her initial frustration had metamorphosed into something much more powerful, a resolve tempered with newfound skill.

As night cloaked the world in velvet darkness, Nadia and Clara rose from their places by the water's edge. The lights between Nadia's hands faded but left behind an indelible mark of progress on both their spirits.

Together they walked back toward Moon Hollow, the rebel outpost now aglow with lanterns, and though she didn't say it aloud, Nadia felt a silent vow take root: she would master this power; she would become what Mirrathia needed.

Moonlight enveloped the assembly at Moon Hollow, draping a silver mantle over the rebels' furrowed brows as they congregated around the crackling campfire. The flames leapt and danced, casting playful shadows that mingled with the surrounding forest. Among the Dawnguards, Nadia sat, her emerald gaze capturing the flickering light as she hung on every word the elders shared.

An ancient among them, his voice a coarse whisper of eras gone by and his hair the white of winter's first frost, leaned into the gathering. With hands weathered by countless seasons, he traced the constellations overhead, his tales resurrecting bygone ages.

"When light and shadow danced as one, interwoven companions, The Order of the Just tread upon this very earth. Their allegiance was to the equilibrium of existence," he intoned, his narrative conjuring images that mingled with the cool night breeze.

His counterpart, a woman whose voice was steeped in the richness of antiquity, continued the chronicle. "Masters of both luminescence and umbra, they wove a symphony of splendor, birthing marvels unparalleled. Their might, it was said, sprung forth from Mirrathia's very core."

Drawn in by the heat and the spellbinding narrative, Nadia leaned forward, her spirit alight with eager curiosity. "Do these storied guardians still walk among us?" she queried, her voice a spark igniting the air.

A knowing look passed between the elders, their gazes heavy with the weight of untold secrets. The patriarch with the snow-kissed locks offered a smile tinged with nostalgia.

"My dear, some tales tell of their retreat into the mists of myth with Bellinor's ascent," he whispered softly. "Yet others hold firm to the belief that they lie in hushed repose, awaiting the herald of a new epoch."

The matriarch's voice, laced with an air that sent shivers down

Nadia's spine, intoned, "And still, there are murmurs of a bloodline unsevered, the progeny of The Order of the Just, slumbering descendants destined to rouse and embrace their ancient birthright."

A shiver of connection jolted through Nadia at these revelations. Was her fate intertwined with these venerable protectors? The prospect filled her with a mix of exhilaration and trepidation.

Captain Grey shifted, his gaze piercing the divide to meet Nadia's, a silent acknowledgment passing between them. "Myths are oftentimes birthed from seeds of veracity," he offered. "Your presence here may be more than mere happenstance."

Clara's touch, warm and reassuring, came to rest upon Nadia's shoulder. "Patience, dear one, for in due course, truths shall unfold," she soothed with a serene smile.

A reflective hush then settled upon the rebels, each absorbed in the stories' deeper significance, while above them, embers rose to join the celestial bodies in their quiet watch over the night.

Under a canopy of stars, the Dawnguard elders wove tales as intricate as Lysara's light sculptures, their voices ebbing and flowing with the cadence of memory. Around the fire, rebels young and old sat enraptured, their faces flickering with shadows and light. Nadia nestled between Clara and Aidan, the warmth of the blaze comforting against the chill of the night.

"Long before Bellinor's curse veiled our skies," an elder began, his voice as gravelly as the mountain paths, "the Order of the Dawn stood vigilant, a radiant bulwark against the darkness that crept at the edges of Mirrathia."

Aidan leaned forward, his eyes reflecting a deep reverence for the Order his ancestors had served. He glanced at Nadia, noting her rapt attention.

"Their armor gleamed with an inner fire," another elder chimed in, her hands gesturing to an unseen spectacle. "Each dawn brought renewed strength to their ranks. Their deeds, mighty as they were, bore witness to the power of light."

Clara's gentle voice cut through the silence that followed. "When Bellinor ascended to power, she feared this light. She knew it was the antithesis of her shadowed rule. So she struck swiftly, her Shadow Keepers merciless."

Nadia shivered at Clara's words, picturing these grim enforcers extinguishing flames across Mirrathia.

The gravelly-voiced elder continued, "Many fell... But not all. Some evaded her grasp, dispersing like rays at dusk."

"Their legacy did not perish," another voice added from across the fire, a young Dawnguard whose armor still gleamed without a hint of battle-wear. "Their valor lived on in whispers among those who refused to kneel before tyranny."

The group nodded collectively, each carrying their own story of resistance against Bellinor's oppressive reign.

Nadia felt a question burning within her as fierce as the campfire. "How did they survive? How did they manage to keep hope alive?"

An elder with eyes like polished agate turned towards her. "They kept hope alive because they believed in something greater than themselves. They believed in Mirrathia and in each other."

Aidan rested a reassuring hand on Nadia's shoulder as if to echo the elder's sentiment.

The young Dawnguard spoke again, "In secret glades and hidden valleys, they trained successors, the first Dawnguards, imbuing them with skills and tales of old."

Lysara joined in from where she sat weaving moonlight into a silken bandage for an injured scout. "We sought out others like us, those who carried embers of defiance in their hearts."

Nadia listened intently as Lysara spoke of how these early rebels gathered under cover of night to share knowledge and strength.

Clara's eyes glistened in the firelight as she recounted how they built their numbers slowly over time. "Every lost soul seeking refuge found a family amongst us."

"And now," Garin's voice emerged from behind them, he had been standing watch over their gathering, "you sit among us, Nadia. The cycle continues. The fire rekindles."

His gaze held weight, the weight of history and hope entwined, and it settled on Nadia with expectation.

Aidan's hand squeezed Nadia's shoulder gently, grounding her amidst swirling thoughts of destiny and legacy.

One by one, rebels shared snippets of their own journeys to Moon Hollow, the sacrifices made and loved ones lost to Bellinor's darkness, all culminating in this moment around the fire.

Nadia absorbed each word like a sponge drawing water from an endless well. Their stories resonated within her, a symphony that began to harmonize with her own untold history.

The campfire crackled its approval or perhaps simply enjoyed participating in this ancient ritual of storytelling.

"The past guides us," Garin spoke again after a contemplative silence had settled over them like dew. "But it is you who must forge ahead. Learn from our tales but blaze your own trail."

Nadia felt a spark ignite within her chest, not unlike the first flicker of light she had summoned earlier that day.

As tales gave way to sleep and rebels dispersed to their tents under the watchful gaze of stars, Nadia remained seated by the dying embers, lost in thought. Aidan lingered beside her; even Garin stayed close by as if guarding a treasure yet to be fully revealed.

Their shared vigil beside the remnants of stories told held a sacredness, an unspoken oath binding them to tomorrow's unknowns.

With dawn came whispers among leaves, a subtle reminder that light never truly vanished; it merely awaited its moment to return.

The embers grew cold as Mirrathia greeted a new day, one that would test Nadia further on her path toward an unwritten future increasingly intertwined with this land and its people.

In the heart of Moon Hollow, under the vigilant gaze of ancient trees, Nadia sat cross-legged, her palms upturned and eyes shut tight. Around her, a circle of Dawnguard elders observed in silence. Talia stood to one side, her presence reassuring yet expectant. The air was thick with anticipation, the stillness punctuated by the rustle of leaves and the distant murmur of rebel conversations.

Aidan watched from a short distance away, his brow furrowed as he witnessed Nadia's struggle. She had been at it for hours, trying to coax her latent powers into life. Her face, usually bright with curiosity and resolve, now bore the weight of her efforts like a mask of concentration and fatigue.

"Remember," Talia's voice cut through the quiet, "focus on the light within. Let it flow naturally."

Nadia inhaled deeply, her chest rising as she tried to envision herself as a conduit for the elusive energy she sought to harness. In her mind's eye, she painted an orb of light as she had done countless times before, but it flickered and faded like a candle in the wind.

Her frustration mounted, an inner tempest threatening to unravel her composure. The orb grew erratic, its form pulsating wildly between dimness and blinding brilliance. Nadia's hands trembled as the energy surged beyond her control.

The gathered onlookers exchanged worried glances as the air crackled with untamed power. Leaves and twigs lifted from the ground around Nadia, caught in an invisible maelstrom centered on her being.

Aidan stepped forward instinctively but halted as Talia raised a hand to stop him. She approached Nadia herself, closing the distance with measured steps.

"Nadia," Talia instructed. "Calm your heart."

But Nadia was lost in her own battle, a silent scream building within her throat as she fought to quell the storm she had summoned.

The light orb exploded outward in a blinding flash that sent birds scattering from their perches.

A gasp rippled through the crowd. Shadows danced across their faces as the light ebbed away, leaving only the echoes of their shock hanging in the air.

Talia reached Nadia and gently squeezed her shoulder, a gesture both grounding and comforting. The touch acted like a balm to Nadia's frazzled nerves; her breathing slowed as if tethered to Talia's own calm demeanor.

"You must stay calm," Talia said close to Nadia's ear. "Your emotions are powerful, yes, but they are not your masters."

Nadia nodded slightly, still grappling with the aftermath of her outburst. She opened her eyes to find Talia's gaze locked onto hers with unwavering confidence.

With each breath that followed, Nadia felt more anchored to the world around her, the gentle press of Talia's hand on her shoulder a constant reminder of support and strength not solely her own.

Slowly, deliberately, she raised her hands again. This time she did not chase after the light; instead, she invited it in with a silent plea born from humility rather than desperation.

The orb reformed above her palms, smaller now and less intense, but steady. It glowed warmly against the cool shade of Moon Hollow's canopy. A collective sigh moved through those gathered as relief replaced concern.

Talia gave Nadia's shoulder one final reassuring squeeze before stepping back to allow her space once more.

Nadia maintained focus on the orb; it wavered at times but did not falter completely. With each moment that passed, she gained more control over its luminance, dimming it intentionally before brightening it once again without losing its form.

Aidan's lips curled into a smile tinged with pride at this small yet significant victory, a sign that Nadia was learning not only to summon but also to master the gifts that lay dormant within her for so long.

The elders murmured amongst themselves now; whispers of approval floated toward Nadia like leaves on a breeze. She sensed their change in attitude but kept herself anchored in the present task.

"See?" Talia said, smiling from her place beside Aidan. "She is learning patience, the foundation upon which all mastery is built."

Nadia heard those words too and allowed them to seep into her consciousness where doubt once resided, a reminder that every step forward was part of a journey much greater than herself.

And there in Moon Hollow's embrace, surrounded by ancient trees and newfound allies, Nadia Calder took another step toward becoming who she was meant to be.

Moonlight filtered through the leaves, casting a lattice of shadows over the rebels' enclave as they trained, planned, and fortified their spirit against the darkness. Nadia watched from the sidelines, her green eyes reflecting the flickers of light from the training fires, a pang of helplessness threading through her as she observed the rebels' deft movements and unwavering purpose.

She had yet to master her own powers, the light slipping through her fingers like water, leaving her feeling more like an observer than a participant in this struggle. Her attempts at weaving light were mere child's play compared to Lysara's artful displays. Nadia's frustration grew with each passing day, and the feeling of being an outsider in this realm only intensified.

A sudden commotion at the edge of Moon Hollow drew Nadia's attention. A scout, breathless and wide-eyed, stumbled into the camp, clutching his side. Captain Grey was at his side in an instant, his face set in grim lines as he steadied the man.

"The village... to the east," the scout gasped. "Ransacked... Bellinor's forces."

A hush fell over Moon Hollow. Clara moved swiftly to tend to the scout's wounds while Garin gathered a small group of Dawnguards to strategize. Nadia stood frozen, feeling a weight settle in her chest. The idea that while she grappled with glowing orbs, real people suffered under Bellinor's tyranny brought a surge of guilt.

Aidan joined Nadia, his expression somber. "This is why we train," he murmured, watching Captain Grey rally the Dawnguards.

"I know," Nadia replied, her voice barely above a whisper. "But what good am I if I can't even summon a stable light?"

Aidan glanced at her with empathy. "Your time will come," he assured her.

She watched as Captain Grey pointed at a map laid out on a wooden table, his finger tracing paths and circling areas with strategic importance. Around him stood warriors whose resolve was as tangible as the swords at their hips.

Nadia's heart ached with the desire to join their ranks, to assert herself not merely as a bystander but as a guardian, a staunch defender of this realm that had transcended its existence as a mere mirrored image. A collective intake of breath rippled through the onlookers; Nadia sensed her fingers tighten, morphing into rigid fists beside her. Encircling her, a radiant orb of purest white manifested, its intensity undulating, gaining in power with each throb.

With the grace of a silent wind, Lysara drew near, her touch as soothing as a balm upon Nadia's tense shoulder. "Nadia, find your calm. Don't let the tempest of your emotions wield you," Lysara whispered with gentle authority. Obedient to her mentor's guidance, the incandescent aura that had bloomed around Nadia began to wane, its retreat as tranquil as the retreat of the sea's frothy edge.

Moonlight filtered through the dense canopy, casting a silver sheen over the faces of Aidan and Nadia. Aidan leaned against a gnarled tree, watching Nadia with an intensity that matched the determination in her eyes. She sat cross-legged on the forest floor, her brow furrowed in concentration as she tried to summon light between her palms.

"You know," Aidan began, his voice soft but clear in the hushed woods, "the Order of the Just spent years honing their abilities. Mastery doesn't happen overnight."

Nadia exhaled sharply, her focus faltering as the faint glimmer she'd managed to evoke flickered out. She looked up at him, frustration etched across her features.

"But I don't have years," she protested. "Bellinor's out there right now, hurting people. I need to be able to do something about it."

Aidan pushed off from the tree and crouched beside her, his green eyes reflecting the moonlight. "And you will," he assured her. "But it's not just about brute strength or immediate control. It's about understanding your power, growing with it."

She considered his words for a moment before nodding reluctantly. He was right; even she could see that much. But acceptance didn't quell the urgency coursing through her veins.

As if sensing her inner turmoil, Aidan placed a hand on her shoulder, grounding her. "Come on," he said with a slight smile. "Let's try again."

Nadia nodded and closed her eyes once more, reaching for that elusive spark within her.

Their training continued through the week, Aidan always by Nadia's side, patient and supportive. Under his guidance and the tutelage of Lysara and Clara, Nadia slowly began to grasp the basics of lightweaving.

One afternoon found them at a clearing where sunlight poured through a break in the trees like liquid gold. Aidan stood before Nadia with an encouraging grin.

"Remember," he said as she focused on the space before her, "lightweaving is about balance and harmony."

Nadia nodded, drawing in a deep breath as she extended her hands outward. This time when she called upon her power, a warm glow emanated from her fingertips, growing steadily into a small orb that floated between them.

"That's it!" Aidan exclaimed with genuine excitement.

The orb wavered for a moment before stabilizing once again under Nadia's newfound confidence.

Emboldened by her success, Nadia attempted to move the orb, guiding it through the air with gentle motions of her hands. The light followed obediently at first but then grew erratic as fatigue set in.

"Don't push too hard," Aidan cautioned as he watched the orb flicker and dip dangerously close to fading out.

"I can do this," Nadia murmured through gritted teeth, sweat beading on her forehead.

The orb stabilized once more and began to move with more purpose as if reflecting Nadia's determination.

Aidan watched proudly but remained vigilant for any sign of strain from his new friend.

After several minutes of successful manipulation, Nadia finally allowed the light to dissipate with a sigh of relief and accomplishment.

"See?" Aidan said with a smile. "You're getting stronger every day."

Nadia returned his smile weakly; despite their progress today, she felt drained. The power within her was vast and untamed, a wellspring she'd only just begun to tap into.

As dusk settled around them and stars blinked awake in the darkening sky, Aidan helped Nadia to her feet.

"You should rest," he suggested. "We'll pick up again tomorrow."

Nadia nodded gratefully but paused before they left the clearing.

Turning back to look at where the orb had danced in the air moments ago, she felt a twinge of something akin to longing, an eagerness to understand this part of herself that had been hidden away for so long.

Aidan placed a comforting hand on her back and guided her out of the clearing towards Moon Hollow where they could find rest and sustenance among their newfound allies.

The following morning dawned bright and clear as Garin approached them during breakfast with news that required immediate attention, a group of villagers seeking refuge from Bellinor's latest assault was en-route to Moon Hollow.

The rebels quickly mobilized into action; everyone had a role to play in preparation for their arrival, everyone except Nadia who felt oddly out of place amidst the flurry of activity.

"You should go help them," Aidan suggested after noticing Nadia's distant gaze toward the bustling camp members.

"I don't know what I can do," Nadia replied, hesitant.

"Anything helps," he assured her with an encouraging nudge. "They'll need all hands on deck when those villagers arrive."

With a deep breath to steel herself against uncertainty, Nadia stood and moved toward Lysara who was organizing supplies near one of the larger tents.

Throughout that day, Nadia did what she could, distributing food and blankets, comforting frightened children with gentle smiles, and found solace in being useful even in ways that didn't involve lightweaving or mirror portals.

As evening approached and tired refugees settled around campfires sharing stories of narrow escapes and lost homes, Aidan found Nadia once again practicing with orbs of light away from prying eyes. She seemed more confident now, her motions deliberate as orbs danced like fireflies around her fingertips.

"You did good today," Aidan said as he approached from behind.

Nadia glanced back at him over her shoulder; despite everything they faced ahead, the looming threat of Bellinor's dark forces, there was an undeniable spark within her that burned brighter than any orb she conjured tonight, a spark kindled by hope and nurtured by perseverance.

CHAPTER FIVE: SYNCED IN SHADOW

After two weeks of intensive training, under Lysara's guidance, she learned to summon orbs at will, each one glowing with an inner fire that mirrored the determination in Nadia's eyes. She moved them in intricate patterns, weaving them through the air with an artist's touch. The Dawnguards watched, their faces a mix of admiration and curiosity as the orbs danced like celestial bodies in orbit.

"You're making progress," Lysara noted one evening as they stood beneath a canvas of twinkling stars. "Your control is much improved."

Nadia nodded, feeling the warmth of accomplishment spread through her chest. With every orb that responded to her command, she felt a kinship with the light, a sense that it was an extension of herself.

Aidan stood by her side throughout these sessions, offering his own insights when he could. Though his talents lay elsewhere, his presence was a constant source of comfort and encouragement.

Next came projecting beams, a skill that required not just finesse but also focus and precision. Clara assisted her with this task, setting up targets around the clearing for Nadia to practice on.

"Envision the path," Clara advised gently. "Let your intent guide the light."

With Clara's words echoing in her mind, Nadia extended a hand toward the nearest target, a wooden dummy draped in dark cloth meant to simulate an enemy shrouded by Bellinor's shadow. She closed her eyes and concentrated on the light within her, feeling it build like a crescendo before directing it outward.

A beam of pure radiance shot from her palm, striking the dummy squarely in its chest. The cloth smoldered where the light touched it, and a cheer erupted from those who witnessed the feat.

"Excellent!" Captain Grey called out from where he stood observing their training. "You'll be a force to be reckoned with."

The words buoyed Nadia's spirits as she prepared for another attempt. This time she didn't close her eyes; she kept them open, locked on her target as she summoned another beam.

Confidence swelled within her with each successful hit. Her control grew more assured as she moved from target to target until each beam found its mark without hesitation.

Nadia was beginning to understand her power, not just as a means to defend but as an expression of who she was becoming. With every flicker of light that obeyed her command, every beam that shot forth from her hands, she felt less like an outsider in this strange new world and more like someone who belonged amongst its wonders and mysteries.

It had been over a month since she arrived at Moon Hollow; Nadia had found a rhythm to her days that extended far beyond the rigorous training sessions. She'd forged deep connections with the Dawnguards, discovering a fellowship built on shared aspirations and the common thread of destiny. The younger recruits had quickly become like family, each one torn from their former lives just as she had been, thrust together into this maelstrom of conflict and camaraderie. What had once felt foreign now felt like home.

Elan, with his disheveled chestnut hair and ever-present smile, was a beacon of light amidst the uncertainty of their lives. One sun-kissed afternoon, as Nadia took a moment's respite, he approached with an easy stride.

"Mind if I join you?" Elan inquired, his hand motioning toward the vacant space on the wooden log where Nadia sat.

"Not at all," she responded, her smile matching the warmth in his voice.

Settling beside her, Elan extended a piece of fruit, a humble offering from his modest provisions. "I've noticed your progress with the light beams," he remarked, sinking his teeth into the crisp flesh of what appeared to be an apple.

"Thanks," she accepted the fruit with gratitude, "Though I'm far from mastering it."

Elan gave a nod of agreement. "Indeed, the path to mastery is long for us all. But it's a path made less daunting when walked together."

Conversations with Elan soon wove into the fabric of her daily life. He introduced her to the others: Lina, whose sharp mind was as formidable as the daggers she wielded; Jorn, the archer whose silence was a veil for his profound insight; and Mika, whose laughter scattered the weight of their burdens like leaves in the wind.

Come dinnertime, they would encircle the fire, their bowls filled with the day's hearty bounty, sharing stories that brought laughter and solemn nods. The younger recruits admired Nadia, who lent an attentive ear to their dreams and tales of yesteryear, her own spirit bolstered by their unyielding tenacity.

Then, as dusk draped the sky in a tapestry of deepening purples and burnished golds, Mika began to hum a melody that felt like it was the very soul of Mirrathia. One by one, others chimed in, their voices a symphony of unity and hope.

"In the land where shadows fall, And darkness reigns o'er all, There's a light that burns within, A flame that never shall dim.

Oh, Mirrathia, land of light, Where hope shines through the darkest night, Together we'll rise, together we'll fight, For the dawn will come, banishing the night.

Through the trials that we face, In this sacred,
hallowed place, We stand united, hand in hand,
In defiance of darkness, we'll take our stand.

Oh, Mirrathia, land of light, Where hope shines
through the darkest night, Together we'll rise,
together we'll fight, For the dawn will come,
banishing the night.

Though the shadows may loom large, And our
path be fraught with strife, We'll press on with
courage, For the light is our guide.

Oh, Mirrathia, land of light, Where hope shines
through the darkest night, Together we'll rise,
together we'll fight, For the dawn will come,
banishing the night.

So let our voices ring out true, In defiance of
darkness, we'll see it through, For in the heart of
Mirrathia, the light shines bright, And together
we'll vanquish the shadows of night."

"Sing us something from your world," Elan coaxed as the last note faded into the twilight air.

Nadia felt a momentary shyness; her voice had never been her pride. Yet the eager eyes that surrounded her dissolved any lingering reluctance. She drew a deep breath and allowed the lullaby, her mother's gift of nighttime comfort about celestial guides and longing for home, to flow from her.

Her voice, tender and sincere, wove a tale of stars and the silent promise they held for weary travelers. The rebels listened, entranced by the foreign yet familiar ballad, its narrative of hope echoing their own silent yearnings.

After the final note lingered and faded, the stillness was palpable, a sacred silence that gave way to rousing applause. Their smiles radiated genuine affection as they celebrated her song.

"That was beautiful," Lina's voice was heartfelt. "You have quite the voice."

"It's just an old song," Nadia's humility shone through.

"But it reminds us what we're fighting for," Jorn's voice was a gentle murmur. "A home where we can sing such songs without fear."

With a nod, Nadia embraced the warmth that flooded her, the unexpected sense of inclusion. Here, amidst this band of kindred spirits, she was no longer the outsider with emerging powers. She had been woven into the very heart of a community united by a collective cause and the blossoming of friendship.

In the soft twilight, Aidan lingered unseen, ensconced within the embrace of the ancient oak's shadow. He observed Nadia's interactions with the fresh-faced recruits, a motley gathering that seldom knew mirth in these fraught times. Their shared laughter, a fleeting reprieve, resonated through the encampment. Nadia's voice, laced with a wistful undertone, floated to him on the evening breeze.

"I've always been enchanted by swordplay," she admitted to her rapt audience. "The way you move, it's like a dance, a dance with danger."

Aidan's unseen smile deepened as he stepped from his vantage point, silent as the hushed breath of the wind.

"Then why not learn?" he offered, materializing within the warm embrace of the firelight's glow.

Nadia's gaze lifted to his, her expression a canvas of astonishment. "I wouldn't even know where to start."

"With me," Aidan declared with a confident ease. "I'll teach you. We begin tomorrow evening."

With wooden swords as their guides, Aidan imparted the rudimentary arts of swordplay. The clearing was bathed in starlight, creating an ethereal training ground where shadows danced with each movement.

"Balance is key," Aidan expounded, demonstrating the proper stance. His feet were shoulder-width apart, knees slightly bent, weight distributed evenly. "Your feet are your anchor. Without proper footing, even the strongest strike becomes vulnerable."

Nadia mimicked his position, wobbling slightly as she adjusted her weight. Aidan circled her, gently correcting her posture with light touches, straightening her back, adjusting her grip on the practice sword.

"Better," he said. "Now, the basic forms. Watch closely."

He moved through a series of fundamental strikes and blocks, each motion fluid and precise. The wooden sword whistled through the air, creating patterns that Nadia struggled to follow.

"Your turn," Aidan encouraged, stepping back to give her space.

Nadia's initial attempts were hesitant, her movements choppy and uncertain. The practice sword felt awkward in her hands, nothing like the weightless light she'd grown accustomed to wielding.

"Don't think so much," Aidan advised, moving behind her. He placed his hands over hers on the sword's hilt, guiding her through the motion. "Feel the flow. Swordplay is like lightweaving; it requires harmony between mind and body."

As he guided her through the forms, Nadia began to understand. The principles weren't so different from what Lysara had taught her about channeling light. It was about intention, focus, and letting the energy flow naturally.

They practiced for hours, moving from basic strikes to simple defensive maneuvers. Sweat beaded on Nadia's forehead, but she refused to stop. With each repetition, her movements grew more confident, more natural.

"Good," Aidan commended as she executed a particularly clean strike. "You're learning quickly."

"I have a good teacher," Nadia replied, slightly breathless but smiling.

Aidan returned her smile, a rare moment of warmth breaking through his usually serious demeanor. "Again," he said, raising his practice sword. "This time, try to block my strikes."

Their wooden swords met with sharp cracks that echoed through the clearing, a rhythmic percussion that marked Nadia's progress from novice to capable student. By the time they finished, the first hints of dawn were painting the sky, and Nadia's arms ached with the satisfying burn of hard work.

Nadia's initial attempts were hesitant, yet with each arcing sweep of her wooden sword, her assurance blossomed. The rhythmic clatter of wood meeting wood broke the night's silence.

On one such night, Garin's solemn figure joined their ensemble, lending a stern gravitas to the training session.

"Remember," Garin intoned, brandishing a practice sword as he aligned himself with Nadia, "a sword is but an extension of your arm, swift and precise."

She watched and learned from Garin's seasoned expertise, each movement devoid of excess yet brimming with intent. She strove to mirror his precision.

Aidan's pride swelled as he beheld Nadia's burgeoning prowess. The fire in her eyes was testament to her unwavering resolve; every stroke propelled her beyond the naive girl who had once traversed the looking glass, drawing her ever nearer to the valiant fighter she was destined to be.

Each nocturnal rendezvous served to refine not only Nadia's martial prowess but also steeled her determination and spirit for the looming confrontations. With Aidan and Garin as her mentors, she was not merely learning the sword's song but also the dance of her own nascent destiny.

Nadia closed her eyes, reaching out with practiced fingers. The warmth of the light responded immediately to her touch, eager to be molded. Her brow furrowed as she focused, and the strands began to weave between her hands, forming shapes from her own world – first a glowing replica of her smartphone, complete with a screen that flickered with imaginary messages, then a miniature laptop that opened and closed at her will.

"What... what are these strange devices?" Lysara asked, her silver-blue eyes wide with confusion as she studied the unfamiliar objects.

Nadia grinned. "Just things from home," she said, making the laptop dissolve and reform into a pair of headphones that seemed to pulse with silent music.

Lysara tilted her head, clearly perplexed. "Perhaps... perhaps we should try something more organic? Something from nature?"

Nadia concentrated harder, and the light shifted, forming the delicate shape of a butterfly with wings that actually fluttered. It hovered between her palms before dissolving into sparkling motes.

Clara watched from nearby, her presence soothing. As Nadia attempted more complex forms, a miniature tree, a flowing river of light, Clara offered quiet encouragement.

Talia stood at Nadia's side throughout these lessons, offering not only guidance for her powers but also for her inner turmoil. The emotional tempests that stirred within Nadia could be both fuel and folly for her abilities.

"When you harness your emotions," Talia said, "you channel them into your craft instead of letting them rule you."

With each lesson in control, Nadia learned to steady herself, to transform frustration into focus and impatience into precision. Her mastery over light grew stronger by the day as she wove it into shields, weapons, and intricate sculptures that danced at her command.

The harmony between mind and magic became Nadia's new dance, a dance she performed under watchful eyes that knew she was destined for great things.

Nadia's hands trembled with a mix of fear and excitement as the news spread through Moon Hollow like wildfire: a Shadow Keepers raiding party was drawing near. The Dawnguards mobilized, their silver armor catching the light of the rising sun as they prepared to defend their home.

Captain Grey's voice rang out, firm and commanding, "Positions, everyone! We intercept them before they breach our defenses."

Nadia stepped forward, her newfound confidence igniting a fire within. "I'm coming with you."

Grey eyed her for a moment, his grizzled face softening. "Alright, stay close."

The rebels gathered their weapons and checked their gear. Nadia could feel the weight of her training coalesce into determination. She had practiced with Aidan, weaving light into protective barriers and honing her combat skills. It was time to put those lessons to use.

Aidan clasped her shoulder, his expression stern yet trusting. "Remember everything we've taught you. You're ready for this."

Nadia nodded, her heart racing as she joined the ranks of the Dawnguards. Together, they marched out of Moon Hollow, leaving behind the safety of the stone-carved sanctuary. Their footsteps were silent but purposeful on the forest floor as they vanished into the foliage that shrouded their path.

The rebels' journey was swift; urgency lent speed to their steps. Nadia kept pace with them, her mind focused on the confrontation ahead. She wasn't just a girl from another world anymore; she was a Dawnguard now, a defender of light against encroaching darkness.

As Moon Hollow receded behind them, Nadia took one last glance back at the encampment that had become her refuge in this strange land. She felt a kinship with these rebels, a bond forged in shared purpose.

With every step away from Moon Hollow, Nadia and the Dawnguards ventured closer to their inevitable clash with the Shadow Keepers.

The forest held its breath as the Dawnguards approached the location where the Shadow Keepers had been spotted. Leaves rustled underfoot, betraying their numbers, and birds took flight at their advance. Captain Grey raised a hand, signaling for the group to halt. Through the trees, the dark silhouettes of the Shadow Keepers were visible, their armor a stark contrast to the verdant green around them.

"Shields up," Grey instructed, and the Dawnguards obeyed, forming a barrier with their bodies and their light-forged shields.

Nadia stood among them, her pulse thrumming in her ears. She remembered Lysara's instructions, letting her inner light swell until it spilled from her palms, forming a shimmering shield of her own.

The first volley of arrows whistled through the air, dark shafts aimed with deadly intent. The Dawnguards' shields flared brighter as they absorbed the impact, some arrows disintegrating upon contact.

"Advance!" Grey commanded.

The Dawnguards moved as one, closing the distance between them and their foes. Nadia stayed close to Aidan, who moved with a fluid grace born of countless hours of practice.

As they drew nearer, Nadia's light shield flickered and waned under a barrage of shadow-infused projectiles. She gritted her teeth, concentrating hard on maintaining its integrity. Beside her, Aidan deflected an arrow with his sword, which hummed with a soft glow.

Then they were upon them, the clash of metal on metal ringing through the forest as swords met in combat. Nadia focused her energy into beams of piercing light that she sent towards the Shadow Keepers. They stumbled back, caught off guard by the unexpected assault of pure radiance cutting through their ranks.

Aidan fought alongside her, his blade dancing in deadly arcs. Together they pushed forward, driving back their assailants with each strike.

"Push them back into the shadows from whence they came!" Captain Grey roared over the din of battle.

Inspired by his words, the Dawnguards rallied. Nadia felt a surge of strength from within as she unleashed another wave of light against their enemies. The Shadow Keepers faltered under the relentless assault; their dark armor no match for the combined might of light and steel.

One by one, they retreated, disappearing into the forest's dark embrace. The sounds of battle died down until only heavy breathing and the soft creaking of trees remained.

The Dawnguards exchanged weary but triumphant glances as they lowered their weapons. Captain Grey approached Nadia with a nod of approval that filled her chest with warmth.

"Well fought," he said.

Nadia's shield dissipated into harmless sparks that drifted to the forest floor. She allowed herself a small smile, the victory was minor in the grand scheme but it was theirs nonetheless.

A foreboding sensation wound its way up Nadia's spine as the clamor of warfare dwindled, an unseen presence tracing a cold path along her back. The feeling was familiar, like when the Shadow Trackers had pursued them into Mirrathia. But this time, it felt closer, more personal, as if the darkness remembered her.

With a deep breath, she extended the tendrils of her perception, probing the ether for the source of her unease. There it lingered, a sinister wisp of darkness, not amidst the verdant sprawl of Mirrathia, but emanating from a place much closer to her heart: the mirror in her bedroom.

The vision came in fragments, shadows slipping through the glass, her bedroom door standing ajar when she knew she'd closed it, a sense of something having already passed through. But the images felt jumbled, like memories playing out of order.

Her eyelids flew open, and she found herself locked in Aidan's inquisitive stare. "Something's wrong," she said, her voice barely above a whisper. "The mirror... I can see shadows moving on it, like something's trying to get through."

A crease of worry formed on Aidan's brow. "Could it be Bellinor?"

Nadia negated with a shake of her head, her voice barely above a whisper. "It's different, this is from my home." She huddled into herself, an instinctive defense against the encroaching chill. "And whatever it is, it's breaching the boundaries."

Aidan caught Captain Grey's eye before turning back to Nadia. "We need to speed up your training," he said, squeezing her shoulder. "If Bellinor's reaching into your world..."

"I know," Nadia cut in, her jaw set. "I have to be ready. My family's there, my friends... I can't let her hurt them."

Talia stepped forward, the nearby torchlight reflecting in her eyes. "You're doing well," she said, "but we'll need to push harder now."

The days that followed saw Nadia immersed in advanced training techniques. By the lake's edge with Clara, she crafted complex patterns of light that danced like living sculptures, her control now precise and deliberate. Aidan's combat drills pushed her limits, teaching her to seamlessly blend swordplay with lightweaving, creating a fighting style uniquely her own.

Under Lysara's expert guidance, Nadia's abilities flourished. She learned to weave intricate shields that could deflect multiple attacks simultaneously and fashion weapons of pure radiance. The rebels often gathered to watch in awe as she created elaborate light displays that painted the night sky with cascading colors.

Yet, even as her mastery grew, an urgent pulse throbbed within Nadia; a pressing awareness of the darkness threatening both worlds she called home. Each day brought new skills, but also a deeper understanding of the stakes.

As another training session ended under the moonlit sky, Nadia's breaths came steady despite hours of practice. She had moved far beyond simple spheres of light; now she could sustain complex formations while maintaining combat readiness. The luminescent constructs she created were testament to how far she'd come, yet she knew there was still more to learn.

Aidan watched from the shadows, his piercing green eyes tracking every movement, every flicker of light that danced from Nadia's fingertips. He stepped forward, his presence like a cool breeze in the stifling tension of the training session.

"Nadia," he said, his voice a gentle but firm reprimand, "you're pushing yourself too hard."

She looked at him, a mix of defiance and weariness in her gaze. "I can handle it," she insisted, even as her hands trembled slightly, betraying her fatigue.

Aidan closed the distance between them, his tall figure reflecting the moon's soft light. "I see your determination," he acknowledged. "It's one of the things I... we all admire about you. But even the ancient guardians knew when to rest."

Nadia's resolve wavered for a moment under Aidan's earnest expression. "I just feel this urgency," she confessed, a frustrated edge to her voice. "If I'm not ready and something happens because I didn't train enough..."

He placed a hand on her shoulder, grounding her spiraling thoughts. "Your strength lies not only in your power but also in your heart and your mind," Aidan reminded her. "Overexertion will dull those edges just as surely as it will drain your magic."

She sighed and nodded, understanding the truth in his words. "Okay," she agreed. "I'll be more careful."

Aidan offered a small smile, one that reached his eyes and softened the usual calculation behind them. "We'll stop Bellinor together," he assured her. "Not by force alone, but with wisdom and patience too."

Nadia returned his smile with one of her own, a promise not to push too hard but to stand resolute in their shared goal to thwart Bellinor's dark ambitions.

Under a sky jeweled with stars, Nadia sought out Talia, finding her gazing into the embers of a dying fire. The flickering light cast a warm glow on her face, shadows dancing in the hollows of her cheeks.

"Talia," Nadia began, hesitance threading her voice. "There's a darkness I sense, reaching from my home world. It's like a cold hand trying to grasp something it lost."

Talia's gaze remained fixed on the fire, but her eyes darkened with understanding. "Focus on the here and now, Nadia," she advised, her tone gentle yet firm. "Your power grows each day. Trust in your abilities to confront the challenges as they come."

"But what if it's Bellinor?" Nadia pressed, her green eyes searching Talia's face for answers. "What if she's reaching through the mirror, trying to..."

"Your concern is valid," Talia interrupted, raising a hand to still Nadia's worries. "But spreading yourself too thin over possibilities will only weaken your resolve when certainty strikes."

Nadia nodded, absorbing Talia's words, though they did little to quell the unease that gnawed at her. She watched Talia rise to her feet, graceful despite the heaviness that settled upon her shoulders.

"Rest tonight," Talia said with a smile that didn't quite reach her eyes. "We'll continue your training at dawn."

As Nadia turned to leave, Talia's smile faded. Her brow furrowed deeply as she glanced toward the direction of Nadia's bedroom mirror in the human realm, a mirror that served as a silent sentinel to their conversations and plans. She could feel it too, the creeping tendrils of darkness that sought out their reflection in another world.

Talia remained by the fire long after Nadia retreated to her tent, troubled by what she sensed yet unwilling to burden the young girl with fears that might never come to pass. The flames crackled and popped as if whispering secrets only Talia could hear, secrets she would keep closely guarded for now.

The morning sun pierced the horizon, spilling golden light over Moon Hollow as Nadia stood at the center of a clearing. She focused on the grass beneath her feet, hands held low with palms facing the earth. Drawing upon techniques Lysara had recently taught her, she attempted something new, using her light to accelerate natural growth.

'Life responds to light,' Lysara had explained. 'Not just as illumination, but as energy.'

Nadia channeled her power differently now, not as beams or shields, but as a gentle, nurturing force. The grass began to respond, growing visibly taller, thicker, weaving itself into a living barrier. Vines sprouted and intertwined, creating a wall of vegetation that could provide natural cover in battle.

But something within Nadia felt amiss, a dissonance in the air that made her skin prickle. Her focus wavered, and the accelerated growth slowed, then stopped altogether.

"Talia," Nadia's voice trembled as she lowered her hands. "There's something wrong."

Before Talia could respond, a sharp gasp escaped Nadia's lips. Her bright green eyes clouded over with a milky haze as she clutched her head in agony. The light that had been at her command snuffed out instantly as she crumpled to the ground like a puppet with severed strings.

"Nadia!" Talia was at her side in an instant, cradling the girl's head in her lap. She recognized the signs of a vision, she had experienced many herself, but this one was different; it was shared.

Their breaths synchronized, and the world around them fell away. They were no longer in Moon Hollow but standing before the old wooden mirror in Nadia's bedroom. The carvings on its frame seemed to writhe and twist as if alive.

Talia watched through Nadia's eyes as darkness oozed from the mirror's surface like ink spilling into clear water. It reached out with tendrils that sought the warmth of their world, desiring to extinguish it.

A chill settled over them both as they stood helpless before the encroaching shadow, a darkness with no face but one they both knew belonged to Bellinor.

The vision faded as quickly as it had come, leaving them back in Moon Hollow with only the echoes of cold whispers lingering in their minds.

Talia's heart raced; this vision was a harbinger, one that tied their fates together more tightly than she had anticipated. She brushed a strand of auburn hair from Nadia's forehead, concern etching deep lines on her face.

As Nadia's eyes slowly regained their natural hue and clarity returned to her gaze, Talia held her gaze firmly, a silent vow passing between them that they would face whatever darkness threatened their worlds together.

Nadia's unwavering resolve manifested in the firm set of her jaw as she stood, the echoes of her vision lingering like ghostly whispers. "I have to go back," she pronounced, her voice ringing with an ironclad tenacity that sliced through the calm of the morning like a finely honed blade.

Aidan moved closer, the tempest of worry in his striking green eyes mirroring the inner turmoil he felt. "It's not safe," he argued, his words weighted with the protective instinct that tethered their souls. The apprehension he felt for her safety reverberated through him, as palpable as the beat of his heart. "Bellinor's shadows could be lying in wait to capture you."

The Dawnguards surrounding them shifted their stance, the soft symphony of their armor's clink speaking of readiness and unease. They too grasped the potent pull of familial bonds, yet they harbored deep-seated fears for the well-being of the brave soul who had become their comrade.

"I need to see my parents," Nadia insisted, her voice firm, her fists balled in determination at her sides. "They could be facing peril because of my actions."

The rebels shared weighted glances, their expressions carved with the stark realization that Nadia's personal quest might very well alter the course of the conflict they were all entrenched in. Captain Grey, his visage a map of hard-won scars, stepped forward to stand shoulder to shoulder with Aidan.

Grey's voice, rough as stone yet laced with concern, carried a heavy admission, "We can't stop you." A pause, weighted with unspoken fears, before he continued, "But we can help prepare you." It was a reluctant blessing, the kind born of necessity rather than desire.

A wave of acknowledgment and unity surged among them, the Dawnguards' solidarity taking shape with the unyielding strength of forged steel. Around Nadia, the air thrummed with their collective support, enveloping her in a mantle woven from threads of camaraderie and courage, each fiber resonating with the group's steadfast commitment.

Clara stepped forward, her presence a tranquil oasis in the midst of a brewing storm. Her healer's hands, tender yet resolute, came to rest upon Nadia's shoulders, a silent promise of unwavering support. "Take this," Clara murmured, the softness of her voice a stark contrast to the urgency of the moment. She pressed a vial into Nadia's palm, its contents aglow with a light not of this world. "It will conceal you from dark seekers for a while, shroud you in shadows even as you walk in light."

On the fringes of this scene, Aidan watched with growing concern. As he witnessed the exchange, a deep sense of unease settled in his chest. The thought of Nadia facing such danger alone went against every protective instinct he'd developed since she'd arrived in Mirrathia. They'd fought side by side, trained together, and he'd come to see her as family, the sister he'd never had.

"We're coming with you," announced Elan, as Jorn, Lina and Mika stepped beside Nadia with unwavering certainty.

Nadia met their gaze, gratitude mingling with fear. Together they turned toward the mirror that served as both portal and omen, ready to face whatever awaited them on the other side.

At the threshold of the weathered mirror, the rebels gathered, an unspoken vow knitting their expressions into a tapestry of determination. Elan's grin had faded into a line of resolve, Jorn's hands rested on his bow, poised for unseen threats. Lina's fingers danced near her daggers, and Mika's laughter had given way to a steely silence.

"We're not letting you do this alone," Elan said, his voice a quiet thunder.

Nadia nodded, understanding their concern. "You can't abandon Moon Hollow. They need you here if more Shadow Keepers come."

"Then at least let one of us go with you," Jorn chimed in, his quiet voice carrying weight.

Lina stepped forward, her gaze sharp as the blades she wielded. "I'll go. I'm quick, quiet, and I know how to stay hidden."

Mika reached out, squeezing Nadia's hand with an earnestness that belied her usual buoyancy. "Just hurry back to us," she implored.

Nadia felt the invisible threads of their camaraderie wrap around her like a protective cloak. "I promise I'll be as quick as I can."

She turned to face the mirror, then glanced back at Lina. "Ready?"

Lina nodded, stepping up beside her. "Let's do this."

With a deep breath to draw in the supportive strength of her friends, Nadia took Lina's hand and reached toward the mirror. As her fingers touched the cool surface, she instinctively created a protective shield around them both—something she'd never tried before. Ripples of light cascaded around them like liquid silver.

"Be safe," whispered Elan as they stepped forward together.

The mirror's surface enveloped them, and suddenly they were tumbling through swirling colors. Nadia felt Lina's grip tighten as they emerged into her bedroom, both stumbling slightly from the transition.

Behind them, the surface stilled once more, leaving their friends in Moon Hollow staring at an empty reflection, hoping they'd made the right choice.

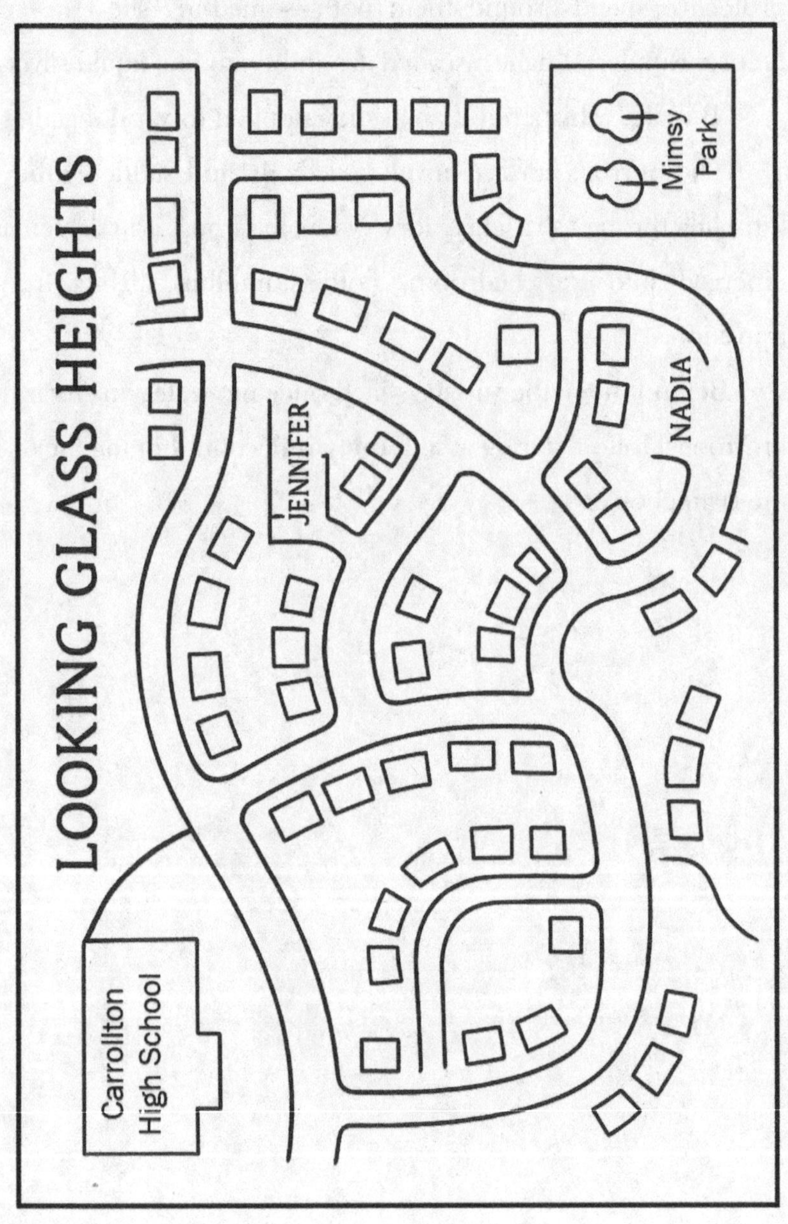
LOOKING GLASS HEIGHTS
Carrollton High School
JENNIFER
NADIA
Mimsy Park

CHAPTER SIX: SHADOWS IN THE GLASS

Jenny stared at the mirror in disbelief, her phone clutched in one hand as she frantically tapped the screen. She'd already posted three SnapLife stories: "MY BEST FRIEND JUST WALKED THROUGH A MIRROR???" with a shaky video of the rippling surface, followed by "HELP WTF IS HAPPENING" and "BEEN AN HOUR WHERE IS SHE???"

Her fingers flew across the keyboard, sending text after text:

Nadia where are you

ANSWER ME

Your parents are home!!!

They're asking about dinner

NADIA THIS ISN'T FUNNY

Each message showed as delivered but unread. She tried calling again—straight to voicemail. Jenny's heart raced as she heard footsteps on the stairs.

"Girls? Everything okay up there?" Sarah's voice called.

"Um, yeah! Just... studying!" Jenny shouted back, shoving her phone in her pocket. She grabbed a textbook from Nadia's desk and opened it to a random page, trying to look busy.

The mirror's surface suddenly rippled like liquid silver. Jenny whipped out her phone again, hitting record just as a dark shape oozed from its depths; an inky tendril that stretched across the floor like spilled oil.

The temperature plummeted. Jenny's breath came out in visible puffs as the shadow slithered past her feet, leaving frost patterns on the carpet. Every instinct screamed at her to run, but she kept filming, her hand shaking.

"Oh my god oh my god," she said, backing away. The shadow seemed to sense her movement, pausing momentarily before continuing its path toward the door.

Just as suddenly as it appeared, the shadow dissolved into wisps of darkness. Jenny stopped recording and immediately posted it to SnapLife with trembling fingers: "SOMETHING CAME OUT OF THE MIRROR" followed by a string of shocked emojis.

The comments started flooding in.

ThunderCat_Vibes: fake af

MidnightScribbler: nice special effects lol

DramaLlama_Crisis: jenny u ok??

The mirror rippled again. Jenny dropped her phone as Nadia tumbled through, accompanied by a stranger. Both wore strange, medieval-looking clothes that looked like they were straight out of a fantasy movie.

"Jenny!" Nadia gasped, scrambling to her feet. "You're still here!"

Jenny snatched up her phone, switching to camera mode. "What... how... where have you BEEN?" She snapped a photo of Nadia in her Mirrathian outfit before Nadia could protest.

"Delete that!" Nadia hissed. "Jenny, please, I can explain—"

"Nadia? Jennifer? Dinner's ready!" Sarah's voice came from downstairs.

Jenny's eyes widened. "Your mom's coming! Quick, change!" She shoved her phone in her pocket and dove for Nadia's closet, pulling out the first normal clothes she could find.

As Nadia changed, Lina examined the room with wide eyes, fingering the edge of a poster as if she'd never seen one before.

"Who's that?" Jenny whispered, nodding at Lina.

"This is Lina," Nadia said, rushing through introductions. "She's from Mirrathia. We need to...".

"Girls? Everything okay up there?" Tom called.

"Coming!" Jenny shouted back. She turned to Lina and thrust a pile of clothes at her. "Put these on and... just... try not to act too weird, okay?"

Dinner was an exercise in controlled chaos. Sarah and Tom welcomed Lina warmly, though they exchanged confused glances at her sudden appearance. Jenny spun an elaborate tale about a last-minute exchange program, while Nadia tried to field any questions about Lina before she could answer.

"So, Lina," Tom said, passing the potatoes, "where exactly are you from?"

"Mirrathia," Lina answered before Nadia could intervene.

"Mira-thea," Nadia corrected over her. "It's a small country in Eastern Europe. Very rural."

Lina looked puzzled at the deception but played along, though her formal posture and the way she examined the microwave with curiosity made it clear she was unfamiliar with modern technology.

"Do you not have these... devices in your homeland?" Sarah asked, noticing Lina's fascination with the dishwasher.

"Our village is quite... traditional," Lina replied, catching Nadia's warning glance.

Jenny jumped in to help. "Yeah, her town doesn't even have Wi-Fi. Can you imagine?" She gave a dramatic shudder that made Sarah laugh.

As they ate, Nadia noticed Lina's warrior training showing through; the way she sat alert, constantly aware of her surroundings, how she positioned herself with her back to the wall. Every sound made her turn slightly, ready for action.

"You seem very... attentive," Tom observed, watching Lina's quick reactions.

"She's just not used to all the noise," Nadia explained. "Where she's from is much quieter."

Nadia, Jenny and Lina helped Sarah to clear the dishes. "Mom, Dad... Jenny and I are going to take Lina for a walk around town."

In the bustling streets of the small town, Nadia, Lina, and Jenny meandered among the familiar sights and sounds, their laughter mingling with the hum of everyday life. Yet Nadia's gaze drifted often to the reflective surfaces they passed; shop windows, car mirrors, puddles left by a morning drizzle. She searched for anomalies, for signs of Mirrathia's encroaching darkness.

"Nadia, Earth to Nadia!" Jenny waved a hand in front of her face, pulling her back from the edge of another world. "You're zoning out again."

Nadia forced a smile. "Sorry, just got a lot on my mind."

Jenny linked arms with her, steering them towards the park. "You can tell me, you know."

As they walked, Nadia watched shadows play across the ground, darker and more persistent than they should have been at this time of day. A chill ran down her spine. She stopped in her tracks when she saw a shadow slither against the natural direction of light.

"Lina," Nadia called, trying to keep her voice down. "Do you see that?"

"See what?" Jenny followed Nadia's gaze but shrugged. "It's just a shadow."

"It's not right," Nadia insisted, but the shadow had resumed its normal behavior.

"I sensed it too. I'll meet you back at your home." Lina slipped quietly into the night, tracking the shadows.

The hours stretched as Nadia waited anxiously in her bedroom, glancing repeatedly at the clock. Just as she was about to text Jenny for help, there was a soft tap at her window. Nadia rushed over to find Lina perched on the branch of the oak tree outside, her face grim in the moonlight.

"Let me in," she whispered.

Once inside, Lina shivered despite the room's warmth. Her clothes were damp with night dew, and a small cut ran across her cheekbone.

"What happened?" Nadia asked, grabbing a tissue to dab at the blood.

"I followed it to the town center," Lina said, her voice low. "It moves with purpose, Nadia, not mindlessly. I watched it circle the jewelry store three times before slipping inside. She demonstrated with her hands, tracing a methodical pattern. Every mirror in there shattered at once."

Lina removed her boot and emptied out small glass shards. She ran a hand through her hair, frustration evident in her tense shoulders. "I tried to intercept it, but it sensed me. These Shadow Trackers are more aware than I expected."

"Did anyone see you?" Nadia asked, worried about explaining Lina's nighttime excursion.

"No. But the shadows are growing stronger. They're not just passing through, they're searching." Lina's eyes met Nadia's with solemn intensity. "We don't have much time."

Golden tendrils of dawn filtered through the blinds, weaving a tapestry of light and shadow across the wooden planks of Nadia's bedroom floor. But morning brought its own challenges. Nadia had to find clothes for Lina to wear to school, explaining basics like zippers and sneakers.

"These shoes feel strange," Lina complained, wiggling her toes in the borrowed sneakers. "And I cannot go without my weapons."

"School has a strict no-weapons policy," Nadia said, watching Lina reluctantly set aside her daggers.

Jenny arrived early, her phone already in hand. "Morning! Oh good, you got her dressed. We should probably figure out our story for..." She stopped mid-sentence, staring at her phone. "Nadia, your SnapLife is blowing up!"

"What?" Nadia pulled out her own phone, which immediately began buzzing with notifications.

The three girls walked to school together, Nadia's phone continuously pinging with alerts.

"I don't understand," Nadia muttered, scrolling through her feed. "I haven't posted anything since..." She froze. Her SnapLife was filled with content: photos of silver-leafed trees, videos of rebels training, selfies with the Dawnguards, and countless shots of Aidan.

"Oh my god," Jenny breathed, looking over her shoulder. "Is that where you were? Who are all these people?" She swiped through the photos rapidly. "And who's the cute guy with your face?"

Lina peered at the screen and gasped. "You captured their spirits in this device?" Her hand flew to where her daggers should have been. "Release them! This is dark magic!"

"No, no!" Nadia tried to explain. "They're just pictures, like paintings but instant. Remember when I showed you in Mirrathia?"

"But they move!" Lina pointed at a video of Elan laughing at the campfire. "His soul is trapped!"

Jenny was already screenshotting everything. "This is incredible! Look at this place! And these outfits! Was this some kind of medieval LARP camp?"

"Jenny, stop posting!" Nadia pleaded, trying to grab her friend's phone. "And it wasn't LARP, it was real!"

"A metal beast!" Lina suddenly shouted, jumping back as a vehicle passed them. She dropped into a defensive stance.

"It's just transportation," Jenny said, not looking up from her phone. "Like a metal carriage. Nadia, seriously, who's the guy? Your secret twin or something?"

"That's Aidan," Nadia said simply, trying to sound casual. "A friend."

"He looks exactly like you," Jenny pressed, zooming in on a photo. "Like, identical. Are you sure you're not related?"

"Pretty sure," Nadia replied with a shrug. "Can we please focus on deleting these posts before...."

Her phone exploded with notifications again. Comments were pouring in.

WildflowerRiot: Is this a movie set?

PixelRebel_3009: Best cosplay ever!

SilverFoxNinja: That guy looks EXACTLY like you!

ChaosQueen_xo: Where is this place???

"Too late," Jenny grinned, already crafting her next post. "This is going viral."

The girls walked into Carrollton High arm in arm, whispering to each other about shadows. Nadia's mind was swirling with visions of light and shadow, barely noticing the classmates she passed in the halls. Lina scanned the halls for potential threats, always on guard. Jenny couldn't help herself; she was still posting to SnapLife.

The corridors of the school were awash with the cacophony of student life.; lockers slammed shut like the echoing booms of distant Mirrathian drums.

At school, Lina attracted attention immediately. She moved with the grace of a warrior; and she rarely left Nadia's side. In the hallways, students whispered and stared.

Throughout the monotonous school day, Nadia remained aloof, disconnected from the classrooms' perpetual motion. She drifted from class to class, her mind a world away, hands automatically jotting down notes she wouldn't remember later. In the starkness of math class, her teacher's monologue on equations receded into a muted hum, while Nadia's gaze followed the stealthy advance of shadows along her desk's perimeter. Her pencil drummed an erratic cadence, drawing curious looks from those nearby.

"Nadia," the teacher's voice pierced her reverie. "Care to solve this one on the board?"

Jolted to her feet, she drifted to the chalkboard, where the jumble of numbers swam before her, a mere pretense of engagement with the task before her.

The sanctuary of lunch brought no solace. Nadia and Lina sat with Jenny and their circle at the familiar spot, enveloped by a whirlwind of jovial banter. Yet, her focus remained ensnared by the aqueous reflection in her water bottle, where images danced and warped in ways that defied logic.

"You okay?" Jenny's whisper was a soft intrusion, her furrowed brow signaling worry.

"Yeah," Nadia's response came as a whisper-thin deception. "Just didn't sleep well."

Mark from their history class approached their table. "Hey, new girl," he said, leaning against a chair. "Where you from?"

Lina's hand instinctively moved toward where her daggers should have been. Nadia grabbed her wrist under the table.

"She doesn't speak much English," Jenny interjected smoothly. "Exchange student. Very shy."

In the bathroom mirror between classes, Nadia saw it, a flicker of darkness that shouldn't have been there. When she blinked, it was gone.

That afternoon, news spread through school about the mirrors in the boys' locker room. Every single one had shattered during third period, with no explanation.

When the final bell rang, she and Lina exited into the cool afternoon air. Jenny had stayed behind for an after-school project, so Lina and Nadia walked home together. The streets were less comforting without her friend's familiar banter.

The day's end was a mercy as the girls hastened home. It was difficult to keep up the charade of Lina's backstory.

Lina asked her, "Do you feel that?" An inexplicable sensation of being watched gnawed at her, an unseen entity skulking at the periphery of her vision.

"Yes. Do you see anything?" Nadia asked.

On high alert now, Lina scanned the horizon for threats. Seeing none, she simply replied, "No."

They didn't see the real shadow that detached itself from an alleyway and slithered silently after them.

The shadow moved with purpose, its form fluid and unbound by physical laws. It trailed the girls at a discreet distance, darting between patches of darkness cast by trees and buildings. It kept to the periphery of their vision; there, but unnoticed.

Upon reaching her street, a backward glance revealed a figure enshrouded by the umbra. It glided with unsettling stealth, its outline wavering as though composed of nothing but shadows and ill intent. Nadia's heart thrummed a frantic rhythm as she grabbed Lina's arm and surged forward, propelled by an urgent need for the sanctuary of home.

She fished for her house keys, mind preoccupied with thoughts of homework and training sessions she'd yet to schedule with Aidan.

As she opened her front door, the shadow hesitated, then melted back into the deeper darkness of a nearby hedge. It watched as Nadia and Lina disappeared inside the house.

Saturday dawned, the usual bustle of the Calder household setting the rhythm for the weekend. Nadia's parents, Sarah and Tom, moved through their routine with practiced ease, gathering keys and lists before herding their daughter and her new friend out the door.

The day unfolded with the mundane cadence of errands; grocery aisles traversed, dry cleaning collected, and the occasional neighbor greeted with a nod or a wave. Nadia and Lina trailed behind her parents, their gazes drifting more often than not to reflective surfaces they passed, a shop window here, a car's polished hood there.

Lina walked with the careful precision of a warrior in unfamiliar territory, her stance alert despite the casual clothes she wore. Her hand repeatedly brushed against her hip where her daggers would normally be, the gesture betraying her unease.

"Everything alright, you two?" Sarah asked, noticing how distracted the girls were as they loaded bags into the trunk.

"Yeah, just tired. We stayed up late talking." Nadia replied, her voice betraying none of her inner turmoil. She offered a smile that didn't quite reach her eyes.

As they continued their errands, Tom paused outside the barbershop. "That's strange," he commented, peering through the window. "Looks like every mirror in there is cracked."

"Must have been some accident," Sarah said with a frown. "Funny, the coffee shop's mirrors were broken yesterday too."

"And the salon," added a passing neighbor. "Patricia said they had to cancel appointments because all their mirrors shattered overnight. Strange times."

Lina's posture stiffened. She leaned close to Nadia, her voice barely audible. "Shadow Trackers. They're hunting for portals."

The family made their way to the farmer's market, where colorful produce and handmade crafts brightened the town square. As they browsed a jewelry stall, Nadia heard a sharp crack. The vendor's small hand mirror split right down the middle, causing the woman to yelp in surprise.

"That's the third one this week!" she exclaimed. "What in the world is happening to all the mirrors in this town?"

Lina's grip on Nadia's arm tightened painfully. She reached into her boot where she'd hidden a small blade, her eyes scanning the crowd with practiced efficiency.

An odd sensation crept over Nadia. A shiver traced its way up her spine like cold fingers on warm skin. She scanned her surroundings for any sign of misalignment in this ordinary world. Lina caught her eye, a silent warning passing between them.

"There," she said, nodding toward a sliver of darkness that seemed to move against the natural flow of shadows. "It's getting bolder."

Behind them, weaving between shoppers, the shadow moved. It slipped from one pool of shade to another, leaving a trail of destruction in its wake. A reflective serving platter cracked at the kitchenware stand. A decorative mirror on a craft table splintered. A puddle that had been reflecting the sky rippled unnaturally.

"We must return to your home," Lina said with quiet urgency. "Your portal must be protected."

"Mom, Dad," Nadia said urgently, "can we go home? I'm not feeling well."

Sarah placed a concerned hand on her forehead. "You do look pale, honey. Let's finish up here."

As they walked away, Lina positioned herself between the shadow's last location and Nadia, her movements subtle enough not to alarm Nadia's parents but purposeful enough that Nadia understood; Lina was shielding her, even without her weapons.

Unseen by the Sarah and Tom, the shadowy figure continued its pursuit always just out of sight, but never escaping Lina's watchful gaze; a whisper of malice lost in the normalcy of a weekend routine, leaving its mark on every reflective surface it passed.

Over the next week, the incidents multiplied. The antique mirror at the downtown boutique cracked overnight. The rearview mirrors on three cars in the school parking lot were found broken. Even the small hand mirror in Mrs. Peterson's purse inexplicably shattered during her grocery shopping.

Nadia began hearing whispers, not from students, but from somewhere else. Faint screams that made her head turn, searching for their source. Shadows moved at the edges of her vision, always disappearing when she tried to focus on them.

At lunch on Thursday, Jenny slid into her usual seat, her cargo pants pockets bulging with gadgets. She pulled out a sleek black case emblazoned with the TechFlow logo.

"Check it out," she beamed, opening the case to reveal an array of shiny tech accessories. "My newest sponsor just sent their whole solar-powered collection. Fifty thousand views on my unboxing video already!"

She fastened a slim silver band around her wrist. "This one's my favorite—solar-powered charging bracelet. Works with any device." She tapped it against her phone, which lit up with a charging notification.

Lina examined the bracelet with suspicion. "More magic from your world?"

"Not magic, just science," Jenny corrected, attaching a small lens to her phone camera. "This wide-angle lens is perfect for capturing those creepy shadows you keep seeing."

"Jenny," Nadia hissed, "you can't post about that!"

"Already did," Jenny said, turning her phone to show them her latest SnapLife story: "MIRROR MYSTERY: WHAT'S BREAKING ALL THE GLASS IN MIRRORLAKE?" The video montage showed various broken mirrors around town, set to eerie music.

"Ten thousand views since this morning," Jenny said, grinning with pride. "My followers love a good mystery. Some are saying it's a massive prank, others think it's earthquakes..."

"It's not earthquakes," Lina cut in, her patience wearing thin. "We should return to Mirrathia before more damage is done."

Later that evening in Nadia's room, Jenny live-streamed herself testing her new solar-powered power bank while Lina paced by the window, scanning the darkening street.

"We should return," Lina repeated, turning away from the window. "Something is hunting us."

"I know," Nadia replied, watching her bedroom mirror intently. "But I can't leave my family unprotected."

Jenny paused her stream and set down her phone. "This is insane. We need to tell someone... the police, your parents, someone!"

"And say what?" Nadia asked. "That shadow creatures from another dimension are breaking mirrors around town?"

"We could start a SnapLife series!" Jenny suggested, her eyes lighting up. "Mysterious Mirror Phenomena Explained..."

"NO!" Nadia and Lina shouted in unison.

On Friday evening, everything came to a head. Nadia was helping her mother with dinner when she heard it... a scream so piercing it made her drop the knife she was holding. Through the kitchen window, she saw it clearly for the first time: a shadow figure gliding across their lawn toward the house.

"Mom, I forgot something upstairs," she said, trying to keep her voice steady. She raced to her room where Lina and Jenny were doing homework.

"It's here," she gasped. "The shadow, it's coming for the mirror!"

They could hear it now, a scratching sound at the window, like nails on glass. The temperature in the room plummeted.

The bedroom door handle began to turn.

"Shield!" Lina commanded, drawing ceremonial daggers she'd kept hidden.

Nadia threw her hands up instinctively, and light burst from her palms, forming a protective dome around the three of them. The shadow creature slipped under the door, a mass of writhing darkness that recoiled from Nadia's light.

It circled them, searching for weakness, then suddenly dove for the mirror. Without thinking, Nadia lunged after it, maintaining the shield around herself and Lina.

"Nadia, no!" Jenny grabbed her arm, trying to pull her back.

But momentum carried all three of them forward. The mirror's surface rippled like water, and then they were falling through kaleidoscopic colors, tumbling between worlds with Jenny's scream echoing in their ears.

They landed hard on the forest floor of Mirrathia, the portal snapping shut behind them with a sound like breaking glass.

CHAPTER SEVEN: THE SHIELD MAIDEN

The silver glow of the portal faded behind them, leaving Nadia, Lina, and Jenny standing amid the towering trees of Mirrathia. The forest floor was carpeted with moss that shimmered with an inner light, casting soft illumination on their faces. Jenny's eyes were wide with wonder, her mouth agape as she took in the impossible landscape around her.

"I can't believe this is real," Jenny whispered, fumbling in her cargo pants pocket for her phone. She aimed it at a nearby tree whose silver leaves tinkled like wind chimes in the gentle breeze. "No one at school is ever going to believe this."

Lina's expression hardened as she watched Jenny snap another photo. "Put that away," she hissed, reaching for Jenny's phone. "Those things don't even work here, and the light could attract attention we don't want."

Jenny clutched her phone protectively to her chest. "But I need to document everything! This is literally another world!"

"A world where we could all die if you don't start taking this seriously," Lina retorted, her hand never straying far from the daggers at her hip. She turned to Nadia with accusation in her eyes. "I still can't believe you brought her through."

Nadia sighed, running her hand through her auburn hair. "It wasn't exactly planned. She grabbed onto me just as we went through." She placed a gentle hand on Jenny's shoulder. "But we'll protect her. She's my best friend, Lina."

Lina's mouth tightened into a thin line. "We need to get moving. The portal opened far from Moon Hollow, and we've got hours of walking ahead of us."

As they began their trek through the forest, Jenny couldn't contain her excitement, despite Lina's glares. She marveled at flowers that unfurled as they passed, their petals glowing with bioluminescence. She gasped at creatures that resembled rabbits but with antlers spiraling from their heads, and birds whose feathers shimmered with colors that had no name in their world.

"This is better than any filter," Jenny murmured, still trying to capture the landscape on her phone despite the strange way the images came out — blurred or too bright, as if Mirrathia itself resisted being captured by technology.

The sun began its descent, painting the sky in hues of amber and lavender that seemed impossibly vivid. Lina's pace quickened as shadows lengthened around them.

"We won't reach Moon Hollow before nightfall," she announced, scanning the darkening forest. "We need shelter. There's an abandoned outpost about a mile ahead. It's not ideal, but it's safer than being in the open after dark."

"Abandoned outpost?" Jenny perked up. "Like, a haunted castle or something?"

Lina's eyes narrowed. "It's a former Shadow Keeper station. They moved closer to the Citadel months ago, but that doesn't mean it's safe. We'll need to be cautious."

As they continued forward, Nadia felt a strange prickling at the back of her neck. She glanced behind them, unable to shake the feeling they were being watched. The shadows between the trees deepened, moving in ways that couldn't be explained by the fading light alone.

"What's wrong?" Jenny asked, noticing Nadia's distraction.

"I'm not sure," Nadia replied, her voice dropping to a whisper. "Something doesn't feel right."

Lina followed Nadia's gaze into the gathering darkness. "We need to hurry," she said, her hand now resting on her dagger hilt.

They quickened their pace, the forest around them growing darker with each passing minute. The once-friendly glow of the flora now cast eerie shadows that danced and shifted. Jenny's excitement had dimmed, replaced by a nervousness that kept her close to Nadia's side.

As they approached a clearing, Nadia saw it; a flicker of

movement too deliberate to be the wind, too dark to be a forest creature. A shadow that didn't belong, sliding between the trees with purpose.

"There!" She pointed, her heart suddenly racing. "Did you see that?"

Lina spun, daggers now drawn and glinting in the fading light. "Where?"

"It moved behind that grove," Nadia said, already stepping toward it. "It's the same presence I felt near the mirror in my bedroom."

"What are you talking about?" Jenny asked, fear creeping into her voice.

But Nadia was already moving, driven by an instinct that overrode caution. The shadow had followed them through—or had it been leading them all along? Either way, it was here, in Mirrathia, and that could only mean danger for both worlds.

"Nadia, wait!" Lina called, but her voice seemed distant as Nadia broke into a run, pursuing the shadow that darted just ahead of her, always visible but never quite within reach.

The chase had begun.

Nadia's eyes darted from shadow to shadow, the golden light of Mirrathia casting elongated shapes onto the forest floor. Trees, their trunks like ancient sentinels, stood watch over her frantic search. Her gaze snagged on a disturbance, a flutter of darkness against the backdrop of gleaming foliage.

She bolted, feet barely touching the ground as she weaved

between the trees. Branches whipped at her face, snagging her hair, but she pushed forward. The whisper of leaves seemed to mock her urgency, rustling softly as if to hush her tumultuous passage.

"Nadia! Stop!" Lina's voice rang out behind her, followed by the sound of two sets of footsteps crashing through the underbrush. Jenny's panicked breathing was punctuated by the occasional yelp as branches caught at her clothes.

"We have to stay together!" Lina shouted, but Nadia barely registered her words.

A glimpse of something, a wraithlike form, slipped between the trees ahead. It moved with an eerie grace that belied its sinister presence. Nadia's heart hammered against her ribs, every beat urging her on.

She surged ahead, lungs burning with the exertion. The forest blurred into a tapestry of green and silver, streaked with the occasional shadow as she raced after the elusive figure. It was a chase against an entity that dissolved at the edge of sight only to reappear just beyond reach.

"What is that thing?" Jenny gasped as she struggled to keep up, her phone clutched in her trembling hand, its camera app still open but forgotten in the moment of fear.

"Shadow Tracker," Lina spat between breaths, her daggers glinting as she ran. "They're Bellinor's spies. They can slip between worlds."

Ahead, a thicket barred their way. Nadia plunged through it without hesitation, thorns tugging at her clothes, drawing lines of fire across exposed skin. She stumbled out into a clearing and halted, scanning for any sign of movement.

Lina burst through the thicket behind her, pulling Jenny along by the wrist. Both girls were panting, their faces scratched by branches and streaked with sweat.

"Are you trying to get us all killed?" Lina hissed, her eyes darting around the clearing.

The air hung heavily with a silence that was near palpable, broken only by the distant call of some unseen bird. Nadia's breaths came in heaving gasps as she circled slowly, senses stretched taut for any hint of the figure they pursued.

A flicker in the periphery of her vision drew her gaze upward. High above in the tangled canopy, a shadow shifted, a darker patch within the dark, then vanished as if it had never been.

"There!" Nadia pointed, but even as the words left her lips, the shadow seemed to disperse like smoke in a strong wind.

"It's gone," Jenny whispered, clutching her phone like a talisman.

Lina stepped forward, her eyes narrowing as she surveyed their surroundings. "No," she said, her voice taut with suspicion. "It's led us exactly where it wanted us to go."

For the first time, Nadia took in the full scope of the clearing. The outpost loomed before them, a stark structure of unnaturally dark stone that absorbed rather than reflected the fading light. Unlike the organic shapes of Mirrathia's natural architecture, the outpost was all harsh angles and imposing walls, its silhouette cutting an ominous shape against the twilight sky.

"The abandoned Shadow Keeper outpost," Lina said, her expression grim. "It's herded us right to it."

"Is that...good or bad?" Jenny asked, inching closer to Nadia.

"Both," Lina replied, sheathing one dagger while keeping the other at the ready. "We needed shelter for the night, but I don't like that it wanted us here."

"We can't go back into the forest now," Nadia said, looking at the darkening sky. "It will be pitch black soon."

Lina nodded reluctantly. "We'll stay, but we'll take watches. I don't trust any of this."

As they approached, Nadia noticed strange symbols etched into the archway above the entrance; angular runes that pulsed faintly with a sickly purple light when she looked directly at them. The door hung ajar, its iron hinges rusted but still functional, as if someone had left in haste rather than abandonment.

Inside, the outpost consisted of two chambers; a larger barracks with empty bedframes fashioned from black metal and a smaller antechamber filled with what appeared to be monitoring equipment. The stone walls felt unnaturally cold to the touch, even for the evening chill, and small crystals embedded in the ceiling cast an eerie, muted glow that did little to dispel the shadows gathering in the corners.

Lina secured the wooden door as best she could, jamming it with a broken chair leg found inside.

"So, is all of Mirrathia this... glowy?" Jenny asked, moving her phone to capture the luminescent moss growing in the corner. "And what are these symbols? Some kind of magic language? Does everyone here have daggers like Lina's? What about those animals with the antlers; are there more weird creatures?"

Nadia smiled despite their precarious situation. "One question at a time, Jenny. The glowing is just how things are here. And those symbols are..."

"Oh my god, look at this!" Jenny interrupted, crouching beside what appeared to be a discarded piece of Shadow Keeper armor. She angled her phone to capture it from multiple angles. "It's like it's made of actual darkness. Is this what bad guys wear here? And what about..."

"Don't touch anything," Lina warned as Jenny reached toward a strange device on a central table, something like a basin filled with black liquid that occasionally rippled though nothing disturbed its surface. "Shadow Keepers leave traps."

The air smelled of metal and something acrid, like lightning had struck nearby. Scorch marks marred one wall where what looked like maps had once been mounted, the remnants of paper curling at the edges as if burned in haste.

"They left quickly," Nadia observed, noticing half-eaten rations and discarded pieces of armor. A helmet shaped like a snarling beast rested on its side beneath one of the beds, its empty eye sockets seeming to follow their movements.

"Too quickly," Lina agreed, her expression grim as she examined faint footprints in the dust; some leading in, none leading out. "This wasn't a planned withdrawal. Something scared them away."

Jenny was examining a strange crystal embedded in the wall, her phone's flash illuminating its facets. "This is so going on SnapLife when we get back. Is this a power source or something? How does magic even work here? Can you teach me to..."

Lina raised her hand for silence. Her body tensed; head tilted toward the door. "Something's outside," she said.

They froze, straining to hear. A soft scraping sound came from beyond the door; the careful step of someone trying to move undetected.

"Shadow Keeper," Lina breathed, drawing both daggers in one fluid motion. "The Tracker must have called for backup."

Jenny's face drained of color. "What do we do?"

"Stay behind us," Nadia said, moving between Jenny and the door. She could feel the magic stirring within her, responding to her fear and protective instinct.

The door shuddered as something heavy slammed against it. The chair leg splintered but held. Another impact, stronger this time, made the hinges groan in protest.

"They know we're here," Lina said, crouching into a fighting stance. "Get ready."

A third blow shattered the wooden door, sending splinters flying across the room. In the doorway stood a Shadow Keeper, his form cloaked in armor that seemed to devour the faint moonlight seeping through the windows. His face was hidden behind a helm shaped like a snarling beast, and in his hands he held a curved blade that gleamed with an unnatural darkness.

Lina didn't hesitate. She launched herself at the intruder, her daggers a blur as she aimed for the gaps in his armor. The Shadow

Keeper parried her strikes with practiced ease, his greater size and strength forcing her back step by step.

Nadia frantically pushed Jenny toward the corner. "Stay there!" she commanded before turning to help Lina.

The Shadow Keeper's blade caught Lina across the arm, drawing a thin line of blood and a hiss of pain. She stumbled backward, momentarily off-balance, giving the Shadow Keeper an opening to advance.

"Nadia!" Jenny's terrified scream cut through the chaos.

Time seemed to slow as Nadia saw the Shadow Keeper turn his attention to Jenny, blade raising for a strike that would surely be fatal. Something in Nadia snapped; a dam breaking, releasing a torrent of power she hadn't known she possessed.

Light blazed from her palms, condensing into a fiery orb that pulsed with golden heat. With a cry of defiance, she hurled it at the Shadow Keeper. The orb struck him squarely in the chest, exploding in a shower of sparks. The impact sent him reeling backward, his armor smoking and melting where the light had touched it.

"Get away from her!" Nadia shouted, her body trembling with unleashed power.

Her gaze fell on a small weed growing between the stone floor tiles near Jenny's feet. Instinctively, Nadia reached out with her magic, pouring energy into the fragile plant. It responded immediately, growing at an impossible rate. Stems thickened and twisted, leaves unfurled and hardened, weaving together into a living barrier that encircled Jenny in a protective cocoon.

"Nadia?" Jenny's voice came muffled through the woven plants, equal parts terrified and amazed.

The Shadow Keeper regained his footing, now warier as he assessed the threat before him. His faceless helm turned toward Nadia, who stood between him and his prey, her hands still glowing with untapped power.

Lina seized the opportunity, darting forward with her daggers. She slashed at the distracted Shadow Keeper, her blades finding the gap between armor plates at his shoulder. He howled in pain, swinging his weapon wildly.

Nadia concentrated again, drawing more light into her hands. This time it formed into searing tendrils that lashed out like whips, wrapping around the Shadow Keeper's arms and legs. Where they touched, his dark armor hissed and cracked, as if the light itself was consuming the shadow-forged metal.

With a roar of pain and fury, the Shadow Keeper tore free, staggering toward the door. A final burst of light from Nadia's hands struck him between the shoulder blades, propelling him out into the night.

Lina was already at the doorway, peering into the darkness. "He's gone," she confirmed, though her voice held a note of caution. "But he'll be back, and not alone."

Nadia stood in the center of the room, her hands still glowing faintly. The rush of power was fading, leaving her trembling with a mix of exhilaration and exhaustion. She turned to the woven plant shield she had created around Jenny and reached out, willing it to unravel.

The plant responded, its stems softening and unwinding until Jenny was visible again, her eyes wide with awe.

"That was... you just..." Jenny struggled to find words, her phone clutched forgotten in her hand. "You made fire with your hands! And the plant... it just grew!" Jenny sat huddled against one wall; her initial excitement completely evaporated. "So," she said, aiming for casual but missing by a mile, "does everyone in Mirrathia have magical powers like Nadia?"

"No," Lina replied, arranging her daggers within easy reach as she prepared to take the first watch. "Lightweaving is rare. That's why Queen Bellinor fears Nadia."

Jenny's eyes widened as she looked at her friend. "Wait, you're, like, special here? That's why that shadow thing was following us?"

"We need to leave at first light," Lina said, her tactical mind already mapping out their next steps. "We'll head straight for Moon Hollow. The rebels will protect us."

Nadia nodded, sinking to the floor as the adrenaline began to ebb. She looked at her hands, still tingling with residual magic. For the first time, she had controlled her power in the heat of battle, channeling it with purpose and precision.

"Try to sleep," Lina advised, wiping her dagger clean of Shadow Keeper blood. "I'll keep watch."

As Jenny settled beside her, still staring at her with newfound respect and wonder, Nadia closed her eyes. But sleep didn't come easily. Every shadow in the room appeared to shift and dance, reminding her of the presence they had chased; the Shadow Tracker that had led them here. And beneath that unease lay a deeper question: why had it wanted them at this outpost? What game was it playing?

These questions followed her into uneasy dreams, where shadows chased her through endless forests and light bloomed from her fingertips like flowers opening to the sun.

Lina woke her companions as the sun was just beginning to rise. "Come on, we need to leave... now."

Jenny and Nadia sat up, sleepily rubbing their eyes. "Why didn't you wake me earlier?" Nadia asked. "You haven't slept at all, Lina."

"There's no time." Lina was already gathering her daggers, her eyes fixed on the doorway. "Our Shadow Keeper friend went back for reinforcements. I've been hearing them moving through the forest for the past hour."

Jenny fumbled for her phone, still half asleep. "Are we in danger? Like, right now danger?"

"Yes," Lina hissed, pulling Jenny to her feet. "They're surrounding the outpost. We need to run, fast and quiet, or we won't make it to Moon Hollow at all."

Nadia felt the familiar tingle of magic at her fingertips as her fear sharpened her senses. "Which way?"

"Northeast," Lina said, peering through a crack in the wall. "There's a gap in their line. If we move now, we might slip through before they close the trap."

They crept from the outpost, keeping low to the ground. The forest was shrouded in dawn mist, silver leaves dripping with dew that sparkled like tiny diamonds. Under different circumstances, it would have been beautiful.

"Stay close," Lina whispered, "and for Mirrathia's sake, put that thing away." She glared at Jenny, who was attempting to film their escape, her phone held out in front of her like a shield.

"But this is incredible," Jenny protested in a hushed voice. "The fog, the colors; no one on SnapLife has content like this!"

Nadia grabbed Jenny's wrist, forcing the phone down. "It'll be the last content you ever post if they catch us."

They hadn't gone fifty yards when a shout echoed behind them. "There! The intruders are fleeing!" The voice was harsh, guttural, like stones grinding together.

"Run!" Lina commanded, abandoning stealth for speed.

They burst into motion, plunging through the forest. Branches whipped at their faces and roots threatened to snare their feet. The sound of pursuit grew louder; heavy footfalls and the clang of armor as the Shadow Keepers crashed through the underbrush behind them.

Nadia's heart pounded in her chest, each beat fueling the magic that surged beneath her skin. She reached for Jenny's hand, pulling her forward as they struggled to keep pace with Lina's nimble form.

"This way!" Lina veered sharply to the left, leading them down a steep embankment. They slid more than ran, sending cascades of loose stones and earth tumbling before them.

Jenny yelped as she lost her footing, nearly dropping her phone as she tumbled. Nadia caught her, hauling her back up with strength born of desperation.

"I'm okay," Jenny gasped, somehow still clutching her phone. She thumbed the camera on, capturing a blurry image of their pursuers appearing at the top of the ridge, black silhouettes against the brightening sky.

"Keeping moving!" Lina urged, already several yards ahead.

They splashed across a shallow stream, the icy water shocking against their heated skin. The crystalline droplets caught the light, momentarily transforming their wake into a glittering trail.

"Look!" Jenny gasped, panning her phone across the scene. "The water's glowing where we step!"

"Less filming, more running!" Lina snapped, but there was a tremor of fear in her voice now. The Shadow Keepers were gaining.

Nadia glanced back, counting at least six armored forms moving with relentless purpose through the trees. Without breaking stride, she threw her hand backward, releasing a burst of light that blinded their pursuers momentarily. Startled cries and curses followed, buying them precious seconds.

"Nice one!" Jenny exclaimed, capturing the flare of magic on her screen.

The forest began to thin, giving way to rolling hills covered in swaying silver grass. Ahead, a ring of ancient boulders stood sentinel around a depression in the landscape.

"Moon Hollow," Lina panted. "Just a little farther."

Their lungs burned, muscles screaming in protest as they pushed themselves to the limit. Behind them, the Shadow Keepers had recovered from Nadia's light burst and were closing the distance once more, their dark armor a stark contrast against the vibrant landscape.

"We're not going to make it," Jenny wheezed, her pace faltering.

Nadia gripped her friend's arm. "Yes, we are." With her free hand, she sent another volley of light orbs arcing back toward their pursuers. The spheres detonated in brilliant flashes, scorching the ground and forcing the Shadow Keepers to scatter.

"The entrance is just ahead!" Lina called out, pointing to a narrow gap between two massive boulders.

They made a final desperate sprint, their feet barely touching the ground. Jenny stumbled again, and this time both Nadia and Lina caught her, half-dragging her toward safety.

"Almost there," Nadia gasped.

The Shadow Keepers were close enough now that Nadia could hear their ragged breathing inside their helmets, could see the gleam of their weapons raised to strike.

With a last surge of energy, they burst through the gap between the boulders. Instantly, shouts of alarm rose from within Moon Hollow. Rebels rushed to the entrance, weapons drawn, forming a protective barrier between the girls and their pursuers.

The three collapsed to the ground just inside the rebel camp, breathing in great heaving gasps, their clothes torn and dirty, hair tangled with leaves and twigs. Jenny still clutched her phone, its screen cracked but somehow still functioning. Lina's daggers were drawn, ready to fight even as she struggled to breathe. Nadia's hands glowed faintly with residual magic, the power still coursing through her veins.

Around them, rebels mobilized with practiced efficiency, securing the perimeter as Captain Grey strode forward, his scarred face a mask of concern and curiosity.

"What in Mirrathia's name happened to you three?" he demanded, eyeing Jenny with particular suspicion. "And who is this?"

Before any of them could answer, a cry went up from the sentries. "Shadow Keepers! Approaching from the northeast!"

The rebels quickly moved to engage the approaching Shadow Keepers, their practiced movements betraying years of guerrilla warfare experience. Archers took position along the high ground while foot soldiers formed defensive lines at strategic points around the entrance.

"Keep those three inside the command tent," Captain Grey barked, nodding toward Nadia, Jenny, and Lina. "Talia will want to speak with them."

Elan guided them deeper into the camp. Jenny continued to film between gasping breaths, capturing glimpses of the rebels preparing for battle; bowstrings being drawn taut, blades glinting in the morning light, determined expressions hardening on faces both young and old.

"Jenny," Lina sighed, too exhausted to be properly exasperated. "Really?"

"Sorry," Jenny replied, not sounding sorry at all as she snapped another picture. "But I'm literally documenting a rebellion in another world. This is going to break SnapLife when we get home."

Lina rolled her eyes but said nothing, her focus already on the approaching threat and what it meant for Moon Hollow. The day had just begun, and already it promised to be one of the most dangerous they had yet faced. "This is insane," Jenny whispered, her voice trembling even as her grip on her phone remained steady. "An actual rebellion. Against actual evil armored knights."

The sounds of combat erupted behind them; the metallic clash of weapons, shouts of warning and pain, the distinctive sizzle of light magic meeting shadow-forged armor. Elan rushed them toward a large tent at the center of the hollow.

"In here," he urged, pulling back the tent flap. "You'll be safer."

Inside, Talia stood over a table covered with maps and scrolls, her silver hair gleaming in the lantern light. She looked, relief briefly replacing the worry that had creased her brow.

"Thank the light," she breathed, moving swiftly toward them. "When the sentries reported Shadow Keepers approaching..."

Her words trailed off as she noticed Jenny, who was now filming the interior of the tent with undisguised fascination.

"An outsider?" Talia asked, her voice sharpening as she looked at Lina and Nadia for an explanation.

Before they could answer, Garin, his face streaked with dirt and blood, staggered up.

"Captain Grey sends word," he gasped. "At least twenty Shadow Keepers surrounding the hollow. More approaching from the west." His eyes darted to Nadia. "They're calling for the Lightweaver to surrender herself."

Nadia felt the blood drain from her face. Around her, the sounds of battle intensified; more cries of pain, orders shouted with increasing urgency.

"We can't hold them," Garn said, desperation edging into his voice. "Not all of them. Not for long."

Talia was there, her presence like a calm amidst the storm, her hand reaching out to steady Nadia's shaking form.

"You're safe now," Talia said, her voice a soothing balm. "Come inside the tent."

Nadia's eyes blazed with an inner fire. "Safe? None of us are safe!" she exclaimed. "The Shadow Keepers... they followed us, Talia. They knew about this place, about all of you. They've been to my home!"

Talia's brows knit together, concern etched into the lines of her face. She placed both hands on Nadia's shoulders, grounding her with a gentle force. "We will face this threat together," she said firmly. "Your fear gives them strength. We must not let it consume us."

Nadia's fists clenched at her sides, the knuckles whitening. "But I have to do something! I can't just stand by while danger looms over everyone here." Her voice rose in pitch as she struggled against the weight of her responsibility.

Talia regarded Nadia with an unwavering gaze. "You have already done more than you realize, child. Your bravery has inspired us all."

As Nadia's agitation grew, a subtle luminance began to flicker around her. It started as a mere shimmer in the air, like heat rising from sun-warmed stone.

"I won't let anyone here get hurt because of me," Nadia declared, the intensity of her words matched only by the light now radiating from her skin.

The glow intensified with every beat of Nadia's frantic heart, expanding outward like a wave unfurling across the sea. The rebels paused in their tasks and conversations, turning their heads towards the source of the growing radiance.

Talia's eyes widened with recognition and pride as she realized what was unfolding before them. The rebels watched in awe as the glow enveloping Nadia coalesced into a shield of light that rippled and stretched over Moon Hollow like a protective dome.

Unaware of her own doing, Nadia had summoned forth a glowing bastion that bathed them all in its gentle warmth, Moon Hollow stood encased in an ethereal shield that shimmered against the encroaching Shadow Keepers.

CHAPTER EIGHT: A DESTINY UNMASKED

"Literally dying right now. This is unreal! Nadia, how is this even possible?" Jenny was filming and talking so fast, she could barely keep up with herself. "Un-freaking-believable! My best friend just made a shield out of light."

In stark contrast, the rebels of Moon Hollow, wearied from their relentless battles, huddled beneath the dome of protection as they gazed up at Nadia's creation. The barrier, alive with dancing luminescence, bathed them in a tranquil glow, its serene patterns casting a mosaic of light over their awe-struck faces. In hushed tones that swelled into a symphony of awe, they traded expressions of astonishment, their voices a testament to the miracle that unfolded within the cradle of their stronghold.

In the midst of the rebels' awestruck murmurs, Talia suddenly stiffened, her face going slack as she crumpled to the ground. Garin rushed to her side, cradling her head as her eyelids fluttered.

'Stand back,' he commanded, his voice cutting through the concerned whispers. 'She's having a vision.'

Talia's eyes snapped open, now glowing with an ethereal blue light that appeared to emanate from within. When she spoke, her voice resonated with a power both ancient and otherworldly.

'Behold,' she intoned, her gaze fixed unseeing on Nadia. "This radiant tapestry spun before us heralds the burgeoning might of our young ally. Watch as Nadia's strength blossoms before us, signaling the dawn of promise that pulses within her spirit."

With these final words, the unearthly glow faded from Talia's eyes. She gasped sharply, body going rigid for a moment before collapsing against Garin's supporting arms. A thin trickle of blood ran from her nose, which she wiped away with trembling fingers as awareness gradually returned to her gaze.

"What did I say?" she whispered, her voice now her own again— softer, human.

Garin helped her to her feet as the gathered rebels exchanged nervous glances, the weight of her prophecy settling over them like a mantle.

Eyes filled with renewed vigor and admiration turned toward Nadia, recognizing her not merely as a comrade in arms but as the harbinger of a brighter future in their relentless campaign against the encroaching shadows.

In the eye of this reverent storm stood Nadia, her breaths drawing deep as she grappled with the surge of emotions that had accompanied her feat. Her fingers, once tightly wound, now unfurled as she regarded the radiant expanse she had conjured, her features etched with an incredulity that mirrored the amazement of her fellow rebels.

With a touch as tender as the first light of dawn, Talia drew close, her hand resting comfortingly on Nadia's shoulder. Her whispers were a balm meant for Nadia alone. "You have called forth this bastion of light instinctively," she murmured, her voice a gentle breeze meant only for the young girl's ears. "This is the essence of your gift, the profound bond you share with the luminous essence that dwells both within your being and in the fabric of the world around us."

In the midst of the awestruck assembly, a sudden silence fell as all eyes turned toward the perimeter where Shadow Keepers had been attacking moments before. Nadia's luminescent shield, pulsing with power, had created an impenetrable barrier between the rebels and their enemies.

Outside the dome, the Shadow Keepers prowled like predators denied their prey. Their weapons struck the shield with flashes of darkness that dissipated harmlessly against Nadia's light. Each blow sent ripples across the dome's surface but couldn't penetrate its radiance.

"They can't get through," someone said, wonder and relief mingling in their voice.

Captain Grey approached the edge of the shield, his weathered face illuminated by its glow as he studied the frustrated Shadow Keepers beyond. After several fruitless attempts to breach the barrier, the dark warriors began to fall back, their shadowy forms retreating into the forest.

"They're leaving!" A young rebel called out, disbelief evident in his tone.

Grey's eyes narrowed. "They'll report back to their masters. This is temporary." He turned to face the gathered rebels, his expression grave yet determined. "But it gives us something we haven't had in a long time... an opportunity."

Only when the last of the Shadow Keepers had disappeared from sight did Captain Grey step onto a weathered crate, commanding the attention of everyone in Moon Hollow. The light from Nadia's shield cast his battle-scarred face in sharp relief.

"We've hidden in the shadows for too long," he declared, his voice strong and clear. "Today, we've been given a sign..." he gestured toward Nadia, "...that the time for action has come. Tonight, we strike at Twilight's End!"

His words ignited a fire within the rebels, unleashing a thunderous cry of solidarity that echoed through their ranks. Their morale soared as they converged upon a broad table cluttered with scrolls and maps, leaning in close as a united front, their determined whispers weaving through the charged air.

The imposing visage of Twilight's End dominated the parchment before them, marked by a sinister sigil that seemed to absorb the very essence of light. The stronghold represented more than a mere outpost; it was a tangible symbol of the Shadow Keepers' iron-fisted rule.

With a practiced hand, Grey traced possible routes toward Twilight's End. "Its barriers are fortified by dark magic, its halls crawling with Bellinor's forces," he stated plainly. "But within those walls lies something that could help us defeat her for good."

Jorn stepped forward, his quiet voice carrying unexpected authority. "The forest will hide our approach until we reach the clearing. From there..." he paused, meeting the eyes of his fellow rebels, "we move like shadows ourselves—silent, invisible, until we're inside."

Throughout this exchange, Nadia stood nearby, her attention divided between maintaining the protective shield and absorbing their strategy. The unexpected weight of responsibility settled heavily on her shoulders, yet she felt a strange sense of purpose taking root.

Twilight's End loomed as more than merely an outpost; it embodied the dread and subjugation that had ensnared the land of Mirrathia. Perched ominously on a barren hill, its serrated parapets cut through the heavens with malevolent intent. The somber stone of its construction seemed designed to leech every ounce of mirth and warmth from the air around it.

In daylight, it stood mute and imposing, a grim warder presiding over a realm bereft of the sun's tender caress. Come nightfall, it metamorphosed into a sinister lighthouse, guiding the vile creatures that prowled and crept in the protective shroud of darkness.

Behind the fortress's formidable embrace, torches sputtered and gasped, their light dim and flickering, akin to stars ensnared within a suffocating cosmic emptiness. The very atmosphere was laden with malevolence, an almost tangible entity whispering threats of anguish and desolation to any who might challenge the ironclad decrees of Queen Bellinor.

As the moment of confrontation approached and courage crystallized within their spirits, the gleam of Nadia's resolute determination mirrored the luster of her shield, casting a radiant beacon of hope amidst the gathering shadows. This night, they would plunge into the very core of that stygian abyss, braving its horrors to land a decisive strike in the name of light; and for the soul of Mirrathia.

Under a cloak of night, the rebel forces advanced toward Twilight's End, their movements as silent as the whispering wind that rustled the leaves around them. Captain Grey led the vanguard, his scarred face set in grim determination as he navigated the familiar terrain. Beside him, Garin moved with the practiced stealth of a guardian who had spent decades evading Bellinor's forces.

The rebels followed in their wake, each step measured and precise. Nadia and Aidan had insisted on joining the attack, driven by an unwavering resolve to stand with those who had become more than allies; they were friends. They moved through the shadows, their green eyes scanning the darkness with identical intensity; their movements synchronized without either one realizing it.

As they drew closer to their target, the ominous silhouette of

Twilight's End emerged against the starless sky. Its towering walls stood unyielding, a testament to Queen Bellinor's reign. The sight of it sent a chill down Nadia's spine; not from fear, but from the cold touch of the stone that reached out and brushed against her senses.

Aidan glanced at Nadia, offering a silent message of solidarity. She nodded back at him, her eyes reflecting the same resolve that had brought them here. Ahead, Captain Grey raised his fist, signaling the group to halt as they reached the edge of the forest's cover.

He turned to face his band of rebels, his scarred visage etched with lines of grim determination.

"This is it," he whispered. "Remember what we fight for; freedom for Mirrathia, an end to tyranny. For our fallen comrades and for those who will rise after us."

Nods and murmurs of agreement rippled through their ranks as each rebel mentally prepared for what was to come. They checked their weapons one last time, gripping hilts and bowstrings with quiet confidence.

Nadia and Aidan exchanged a glance; a silent promise exchanged between friends whose bond had been forged in both worlds they now sought to protect. Together with their comrades-in-arms, they waited for Captain Grey's signal to begin their audacious assault on Twilight's End.

The rebels slipped through the darkness like phantoms, their steps muffled by the mossy earth. Aidan led a contingent to the eastern wall, where shadows clung like a second skin, offering concealment. Nadia followed, her pulse quickening with every step toward the outpost.

Aidan reached into the folds of his cloak and withdrew a small, shimmering orb that cast a faint glow. With deft fingers, he twisted it, and the light snuffed out, replaced by tendrils of shadow that reached up and enveloped the wall. They coiled around the stone, softening it until it became as pliable as clay.

Nadia watched in awe as Aidan motioned for her to step forward. He nodded toward the wall, now dark and yielding.

"Your turn," he murmured.

She hesitated for only a moment before extending her hand toward the wall. Focusing on the light within her, she felt it surge forward at her command. Strands of luminescence danced from her fingertips, weaving into the shadowy tendrils. Where light met dark, the wall began to dissolve.

They worked in tandem... Aidan's shadows creating openings, Nadia's light solidifying their path until a narrow passage revealed itself. One by one, they slipped through into the heart of Twilight's End.

Inside the outpost, chaos was their ally. Rebels fanned out, each tasked with a critical role in dismantling the Shadow Keepers' operations. Nadia and Aidan found themselves in a chamber lined with shelves of dark artifacts and tomes.

Nadia reached out to a particularly malevolent-looking object, sensing its oppressive energy. Before she could touch it, Aidan's hand closed over hers.

"Allow me," he said softly.

He lifted the object with care, his other hand weaving shadows around it until it appeared no more threatening than a mundane stone.

"Keep watch," he instructed as he worked his way down the shelf.

Nadia turned her attention to the room's entrance, her senses alert for any sign of approaching Shadow Keepers. She raised her hands slightly, ready to weave protective light at a moment's notice.

Aidan continued his task with meticulous precision, each movement calculated to neutralize the dark magic suffusing the objects before him. They moved together through the chamber; a symphony of light and shadow, as they sought to disrupt every facet of the Shadow Keepers' sinister machinations.

In the heart of Twilight's End, the air crackled with latent energy, the walls pulsing with a sinister beat. Nadia and Aidan found themselves in a corridor, their exit cut off by the arrival of Shadowguard, elite enforcers cloaked in armor that seemed to swallow the weak light.

Nadia's breath came quick and shallow, her back pressing against Aidan's. They formed an island in a sea of encroaching darkness. The Shadowguard advanced, their movements synchronized and silent, save for the faint clink of their blackened mail.

"Stay close," Aidan said, his voice a steady drum against the rising tide of her heartbeat.

She nodded, feeling the warmth from his back seep into hers, a strange comfort amidst the danger. Nadia reached deep within herself, drawing forth the power that had awakened in Moon Hollow.

Light surged through her veins like liquid fire, radiating outward in waves that pushed back the encroaching shadows. The corridor brightened as if struck by dawn, the walls themselves seeming to absorb and reflect her power.

Aidan's response was immediate and instinctive. The darkness around them coalesced, twisting into his control like living ink. Shadow tendrils writhed around his arms, extending his reach beyond physical limits. The Shadowguard hesitated, their formation faltering as they faced powers that mirrored their own but burned with purpose rather than malice.

The first of the Shadowguard lunged forward, blade aimed for Nadia's heart. She thrust her palm outward, and a beam of concentrated light struck the attacker squarely in the chest. His armor sizzled and warped, steam rising from the metal as he stumbled backward with an inhuman shriek.

Aidan wove his shadows into whip-like extensions that lashed around another assailant's legs, yanking him off-balance before solidifying into bonds that trapped him against the stone floor. Where Nadia's light scorched and repelled, Aidan's shadows ensnared and immobilized.

They fought with a synchronicity that defied their brief acquaintance. When Nadia advanced, light streaming from her fingertips in arcs that cut through the darkness, Aidan was there to catch the counterattack with a wall of shadows that absorbed the blow. When Aidan sent tendrils of darkness skittering along the floor to trip their enemies, Nadia followed with blinding flashes that disoriented those still standing.

A grunt behind her alerted Nadia to Aidan's struggle with a Shadowguard who had slipped past his defenses. Without thinking, she spun around, hands outstretched. A sheet of light materialized between Aidan and the descending blade, so bright that the metal began to melt upon contact.

Aidan seized the moment, darkness coiling around the Shadowguard's throat and limbs until he collapsed, his form dissolving into wisps of shadow that scattered like ash in the wind.

Their momentary victory was short-lived. A massive figure emerged from the end of the corridor; a Shadowguard commander whose armor gleamed with an unnatural sheen. Dark energy roiled around his two-handed blade as he charged forward with a roar that shook dust from the ceiling.

Nadia felt fear lance through her confidence. This enemy radiated power unlike the others—a concentrated darkness that drank in her light. She raised her hands, summoning every ounce of power she could muster. Beside her, Aidan did the same, shadows gathering around him like a storm cloud.

The commander swung his blade in a devastating arc aimed to cut them both down. Nadia's light and Aidan's shadow surged forward independently, meeting the dark blade in a clash of energies that sent them both staggering backward.

"It's not enough," Aidan gasped, his face strained with effort as he reinforced his shadow barrier.

The commander laughed, a sound like stones grinding together, and raised his weapon for another strike. Desperate, Nadia reached out blindly and caught Aidan's hand in hers.

The contact was electric. Their powers, previously separate currents, suddenly merged into something entirely new. Light and shadow spiraled around their joined hands, neither canceling the other but instead amplifying, transforming. The energy surged up their arms and across their bodies until they stood at the center of a maelstrom of power that was neither light nor shadow but something transcendent.

The commander faltered, his advance halted by the impossible sight before him. The combined energy erupted outward in a silent explosion that filled the corridor with blinding, pulsing waves. Where light touched shadow, reality itself seemed to bend and warp.

The Shadowguard commander stared down in horror as his armor began to dissolve, light and shadow eating through the magical protections like acid through paper. His form wavered, edges blurring as the combined power tore at the very essence of his being. Around him, the remaining Shadowguard experienced the same fate; their bodies breaking apart into motes of darkness that scattered and vanished in the face of this unprecedented force.

The energy continued to build until it released in a thunderous boom that knocked Nadia and Aidan off their feet, sending them tumbling in opposite directions as their hands tore apart. The shockwave rippled outward, traveling through stone and air alike.

Then, silence. The corridor stood empty, no trace remaining of the Shadowguard army that had surrounded them moments before.

Nadia pushed herself up on trembling arms, her ears ringing from the blast. Across from her, Aidan looked equally stunned, his eyes wide with disbelief as he stared at his own hand.

"What was that?" he whispered, his voice barely audible in the sudden stillness.

Nadia shook her head, words failing her. What they had unleashed went beyond her understanding, beyond anything she had thought possible. It wasn't just their powers combined—it was something entirely new, something that should not exist.

And somewhere deep inside, a voice whispered that this was only the beginning.

In the aftermath of the battle, the halls of Twilight's End echoed with stunned silence. The rebels gathered in small clusters, their voices hushed as they recounted what they had witnessed... or rather, what they hadn't.

"One moment they were there," a young soldier told his comrades, "and the next... gone. Like shadows at noon."

"I heard a sound," another added, "like thunder trapped inside stone. Then a wave of... something... knocked me clear off my feet."

Captain Grey surveyed the captured outpost, his weathered face betraying little of his thoughts as he issued orders. "Jorn, Lina," he called out to two figures who stepped forward. "You and a select few will hold this position. No Shadow Keeper returns here alive."

Jorn nodded solemnly, his bow clutched tightly in his hand while Lina adjusted her daggers with a determined glint in her eye. They understood the strategic value of their new foothold in Bellinor's territory.

As the main force prepared to depart, Grey's gaze fell on Nadia and Aidan. The two stood apart from the others, speaking in low tones, their faces still pale from exertion. He approached them with measured steps.

"Whatever you two did," he said quietly, "it turned the tide. We'll speak of it when we return to Moon Hollow."

The journey back through the forest was unlike any march the rebels had experienced before. Victory lightened their steps, and for once, they didn't fear pursuit. The Shadow Keepers who had survived had fled in disarray, their ranks broken by forces they couldn't comprehend.

"Did you see them run?" Elan laughed, his youthful face alight with triumph as he walked beside Nadia. "Like rabbits before a hawk!"

"I didn't see what caused it," Mika admitted, her curiosity evident. "I was pinned down near the eastern corridor. One moment we were fighting for our lives, the next... a blinding flash and that boom that knocked us all down."

The rebels traded theories as they walked, their voices rising and falling in the night air. Some claimed it was a trap that had backfired on the Shadow Keepers, others suggested ancient magic awakened within Twilight's End itself.

Halfway back to Moon Hollow, when they stopped to rest briefly, Garin approached Nadia and Aidan. His keen eyes had missed little during the battle's aftermath.

"Your hands," he observed, nodding toward the faint marks that encircled both their wrists; identical patterns like branching lightning, still visible hours after the event. "I've seen such markings before, in the old texts."

Aidan glanced down at his wrist, then at Nadia's. "What does it mean?"

Before Garin could answer, another rebel approached them, eyes wide with revelation. "It was you two, wasn't it? When the commander cornered us in the west wing, I saw a flash of light and darkness together before I blacked out."

The murmur spread through the resting rebels like wildfire, all eyes turning toward Nadia and Aidan. Captain Grey moved to stand beside them, his presence a buffer against the sudden attention.

"What matters is that we won," he declared, his authoritative voice cutting through the speculation. "Twilight's End is ours. We'll sort out the how of it later."

But the seed had been planted. As they resumed their march toward Moon Hollow, the rebels' glances toward Nadia and Aidan carried new weight; a mixture of awe, gratitude, and the first stirrings of something that felt uncomfortably like reverence.

"I don't like this," Nadia whispered to Aidan as they walked. "I barely understand what happened myself."

Aidan nodded, his expression troubled. "When our powers combined... it was like nothing I've felt before. Like we unlocked something that was always there, waiting."

Back at Moon Hollow, the atmosphere was thick with anticipation. Rebels milled about, tending to the wounded and repairing what little they could after the recent skirmish.

Jenny wavered between being helpful and taking photos... her attachment to her phone and other electronic devices confused and bewildered the rebels around her.

The forest thinned as the heroes approached Moon Hollow, the familiar ring of guardian stones visible in the distance.

Jenny rushed forward, her phone forgotten for once as she flung her arms around Nadia. "You're okay! Clara wouldn't let me leave to come after you... Talia had another vision!"

Talia stood more sedately, but her eyes were fixed on Nadia and Aidan with an intensity that made them both shift uncomfortably. There was recognition in her gaze, as if she was seeing something beyond their physical forms; something she had been waiting for.

As the rebels filed into the safety of their camp, trading greetings with those who had stayed behind, Talia approached. Her voice, when she spoke, was pitched for Nadia and Aidan's ears alone.

"Come to the council tent," she said. "It's time you learned the truth."

Jenny started to follow, but Talia placed a gentle hand on her shoulder. "Not you, dear one. Not yet."

"But..." Jenny began to protest.

"It's okay," Nadia assured her friend. "I'll tell you everything after."

As Jenny reluctantly backed away, Nadia and Aidan exchanged a glance before following Talia. The revelation they were about to receive would forever change how they understood themselves and each other; a truth hidden beneath the surface of their lives like a current running beneath still water, invisible until disturbed.

In the heart of the encampment, within the largest tent that served as a council chamber, Talia stood before Nadia and Aidan. The fabric walls felt like they were closing in around them, as if to guard the secrets soon to be spilled.

"You both have felt it, haven't you?" Talia began, her voice soft yet unwavering. "A connection to this land, a pull towards something greater than yourselves." She paced slowly before them, her eyes reflecting the flicker of torchlight.

Nadia nodded, her heart quickening with each word. Aidan's posture straightened, his instincts honing in on the gravity of Talia's tone.

"Your lives began not as you've known them," Talia continued, locking eyes first with Nadia and then with Aidan. "You were born here in Mirrathia, children of King Alaric and Queen Valora."

Nadia's breath hitched; Aidan felt the ground beneath him shift. Talia held up a hand to still their burgeoning questions.

"Your birth was shrouded in secrecy for your protection. A prophecy foretold that twins of royal blood would rise to challenge Bellinor's darkness," she said. "Knowing this, your parents hid your existence from all but a trusted few."

She turned toward Nadia. "When Bellinor's power grew menacingly close, it was foreseen that one must grow away from Mirrathia's shadows. Thus, you were sent to the human realm." Talia's gaze softened as she watched understanding dawn on Nadia's face.

"And you, Aidan," she said, directing her attention to him, "were raised in isolation here, your identity kept secret even as your powers over light and shadow were nurtured."

The revelation hung heavy in the air; two lives intertwined by destiny now laid bare before them.

Talia reached out, taking each of their hands in hers. "King Alaric and Queen Valora disappeared not long after your separation," she explained gently. "Mirrathia was left to believe its heirs lost forever."

She released their hands and stepped back. "But here you stand; the lost children of Mirrathia returned." Talia paused for a moment to let them absorb her words.

"That is your truth," she finished quietly. "The path ahead is yours to choose."

Questions flooded the space between the twins like a relentless tide, crashing over Talia's revelations.

"But how?" Nadia's voice was a mixture of wonder and disbelief. "How could we not know, not feel the truth?"

Aidan, whose mind always ran on tracks of logic, pressed for clarity. "And our parents, the king and queen, where are they now?"

Talia's expression bore the weight of years spent in silent guardianship over such secrets. "The magic that concealed your heritage was powerful, designed to protect you until the time was right. As for the king and queen," she sighed, her gaze falling to the woven rug beneath their feet, "their fate remains unknown."

Aidan and Nadia exchanged a look that spoke volumes; they

were each other's mirror in more ways than one. The longing for answers etched into their faces was mirrored in the other.

Nadia ran a hand through her hair, a gesture of frustration she'd come to know well. "And this prophecy," she prodded further, "what does it say exactly?"

Talia retrieved a weathered scroll from a nearby table and unfurled it with reverence. "It speaks of twins born under the Veil of Eclipse, harbinger of change and balance." Her finger traced the ancient script as she read. "Together, they shall stand at the crossroads of light and shadow to reclaim the heart of Mirrathia."

Aidan's jaw set firm, his analytical mind already dissecting each word for meaning. "So our very birth is a threat to Bellinor," he deduced.

Nadia felt a knot form in her stomach. The gravity of their birthright loomed over her like an insurmountable mountain.

Talia nodded solemnly at Aidan's words. "Yes, which is why you must tread carefully. Your powers combined are formidable but untamed."

Silence fell upon them as they each grappled with the enormity of their lineage. They stood at the precipice of destiny, where every choice now carried the weight of a kingdom on its shoulders.

Nadia looked to Aidan, her eyes reflecting both fear and resolve. "Can we do this?" she asked.

Aidan took in his sister's anxious visage, a mirror to his own turmoil, and squared his shoulders. "We have to," he replied with quiet determination.

The knowledge that their very existence was interwoven with Mirrathia's fate bound them together with new purpose. As they absorbed the full implications of their birthright, Nadia and Aidan understood that their fight against Bellinor was no longer just about aiding the rebellion; it was about reclaiming their stolen past and fulfilling a destiny written in stars long before they drew breath.

CHAPTER NINE: DARKNESS IN RETREAT

In the hushed confines of a tent at Moon Hollow, the twins sat side by side, the air thick with the weight of their newfound identities. Nadia's fingers plucked absentmindedly at the hem of her tunic, a physical manifestation of her internal unrest. Aidan, ever the stoic, stared into the middle distance, his mind awhirl with strategy and consequence.

"You realize what this means?" Nadia's voice broke through their shared silence, her green eyes searching Aidan's for something; reassurance, perhaps, or solidarity.

Aidan nodded. "It means we lead not just as allies but as siblings, heirs. Our claim to Mirrathia's throne is both our weapon and our shield."

Nadia considered his words, the truth of them settling in her chest like a stone. "And our target," she murmured.

"Yes," Aidan agreed, "Bellinor won't stop until she crushes any threat to her rule. And now we are that threat."

Jenny burst into the tent, phone in hand, "I knew it! No wonder he looks just like you! OMG, my best friend is royalty."

"Jenny, were you listening outside the tent?" Talia asked as she headed for the door.

"It's okay, Talia, we've got this" reassured Nadia.

Aidan laughed, the seriousness of the moment broken by Jenny's enthusiasm. "Hello Jenny, I don't believe we've been formally introduced. I'm Nadia's twin brother, Aidan, heir to the throne of Mirrathia."

"Ha, ha, ha. Very funny, Aidan" Jenny said while pushing him aside. "Nadia, no one at home is going to believe this!"

"Oh wow, home... my parents... YOUR parents! Jenny... stop recording everything!" Nadia sighed. She was used to Jenny putting a phone in her face every time something exciting happened, but this was too much.

"I need to get you back home," Nadia said, turning to Jenny. "It's too dangerous for you here."

"Are you kidding? I'm not missing the final showdown!" Jenny protested, clutching her phone.

Aidan shared a look with Nadia. "The battle ahead is no place for someone without training or powers."

"He's right," Garin added, stepping into the tent. "I can open a portal to send you back safely before we march on the Citadel."

Jenny's shoulders slumped, but a spark of understanding crossed her face. "Fine. But you better come back in one piece, Nadia Calder...or should I say, Princess Nadia of Mirrathia."

Nadia hugged her friend tightly. "I promise."

After seeing Jenny safely home, the twins returned to find the rebels preparing for battle. The camp buzzed with activity. The rebels' spirits soared on the wings of their recent triumph, and the news of royal heirs in their midst only fanned the flames of their fervor. They had faced darkness and emerged victorious; now they dared to dream of freedom.

Captain Grey convened with his lieutenants, maps of Mirrathia spread before them like a challenge to be met head-on. His gaze lifted to meet those gathered around him. "The Midnight Citadel," he announced, his voice carrying an edge of steel sharpened by years of resistance. "It stands as Bellinor's heart of darkness, and we shall be the light that pierces it."

A murmur rippled through the group, determination etched on every face. Here were warriors who had tasted victory and hungered for its return.

Garin approached Nadia and Aidan, his expression one of quiet confidence. "The people will rally behind you," he said. "You are symbols of hope; the dawn after a long night."

Nadia exhaled slowly, letting Garin's words wash over her like a balm. She glanced at Aidan once more and found resolve mirrored back at her.

Aidan stood abruptly, pulling Nadia up beside him. Together they stepped from the tent into the burgeoning light of dawn that bathed Moon Hollow in hues of promise.

"The Midnight Citadel," Aidan declared to those who gathered around them. "We will reclaim it for Mirrathia." The rebels cheered, their voices rising in a crescendo that seemed to shake the very ground beneath them.

Energized by victory and united under their true leaders, they began to forge plans for what they hoped would be the final assault; a daring gambit to end Bellinor's reign and restore light to Mirrathia's throne.

As Nadia and Aidan stood before the fire, Talia's gaze locked onto them, her eyes shimmering with a solemn luminescence that spoke of the gravity of the task ahead. She pivoted to confront the twins, her movements fluid and purposeful, the very air around her seeming to hum with the weight of her words.

"Aidan, Nadia," Talia intoned, her voice resonating like a chord struck on the harp of fate, echoing the heavy atmosphere that enshrouded them. "To engage Bellinor within the confines of that profaned fortress is to embark on a trial of the most arduous nature, the likes of which you have not yet encountered."

She paused, allowing the weight of her warning to settle upon the twins like a mantle, its silent presence speaking volumes more than words could ever convey. "The Midnight Citadel is not merely a physical stronghold, but a manifestation of Bellinor's darkest desires and most twisted ambitions. Within its walls, reality itself bends to her will, and the very shadows themselves become her allies."

Talia's gaze softened, a flicker of compassion breaking through the solemnity of her expression. "But remember, your strength lies not only in your individual powers, but in the unbreakable bond you share as siblings, as the true heirs of Mirrathia. Together, you possess the light and the resolve to pierce through the darkness and reclaim what was lost."

A hush enveloped the trio, the gravity of the moment settling upon them like a tangible presence. Nadia and Aidan exchanged a glance, their eyes conveying a silent understanding and determination. They knew that the path ahead would test them in ways they had never been tested before, but they also knew that they could not turn back now.

The rebels worked through the night, sharpening blades and fletching arrows. Nadia sat by the fire, watching the dance of flames as Lysara approached.

"Your light will be tested today," the lightweaver said, settling beside her. "But remember, true power comes not from how brightly you burn, but from how steadily."

Aidan joined them, his expression solemn. "What if we fail?"

"We won't," Nadia replied, her voice stronger than she felt. "Not together."

The Midnight Citadel loomed ahead, a twisted shadow against the sky. Once it had been the beautiful Palace of Light, but Bellinor had corrupted it, turning its bright towers into jagged spikes that looked like they were trying to tear holes in the clouds. Where rainbow light had once danced through crystal windows, now only a sickly green glow pulsed from within, making the whole structure seem alive and hungry.

Nadia shivered as she looked up at it. This place had been her family's home, once. Now it was barely recognizable; like a beautiful face distorted by hatred.

The twins turned to face the Midnight Citadel, their hearts steeled with the knowledge that the fate of Mirrathia rested upon their shoulders. As they took their first steps towards the darkened fortress, they could feel the weight of their destiny urging them forward, guiding them towards the ultimate confrontation that would decide the future of the realm.

Nadia could still hear Talia's words echoing in her head. "Aidan, Nadia," she intoned, her voice resonating like a chord struck on the harp of fate, echoing the heavy atmosphere that enshrouded them, "to engage Bellinor within the confines of that profaned fortress is to embark on a trial of arduous nature, the likes of which you have not yet encountered."

Under the shroud of night, a cloak of silence draped over the rebel forces as they advanced toward the Midnight Citadel. Nadia's heart raced, a symphony of anticipation and resolve playing within her chest. Beside her, Aidan moved with purpose, his eyes reflecting the moonlight that dared to pierce the veil of darkness surrounding them.

The twins led the charge, their steps synchronized with the rhythmic march of Dawnguards behind them. They had become the beating heart of the rebellion, the pulse that drove their comrades forward into the jaws of peril.

As they neared the outer defenses of the Citadel, a whisper ran through their ranks. With a nod from Captain Grey, a silent signal passed between them. In an instant, they scattered like shards of light cast by a prism, each faction moving to dismantle a piece of Bellinor's dark stronghold.

Shadow Keepers, clad in armor that appeared to swallow light whole, emerged from their posts. The clang of steel broke the stillness as rebels clashed with these enforcers of darkness. Nadia drew her sword, light weaving into its blade until it hummed with power. Aidan stood back-to-back with her, his own weapon drawn, shadow and light intertwining around them in a deadly dance.

Arrows sliced through the air from Jorn's bow, finding their marks with deadly precision. Lina darted through the chaos, her daggers a blur as she danced past enemy lines. Each strike from her was swift and sure, each movement poetry in motion.

Captain Grey's voice cut through the din of battle like a clarion call. "Push forward!" he roared. The rebels responded in kind, their determination unyielding as they pressed on against an enemy that knew no mercy.

Nadia felt her powers surge as she parried and struck with an elegance born of necessity. The light she conjured now seemed an extension of her very will. Beside her, Aidan's shadows snaked outwards, ensnaring foes in tendrils of darkness.

The outer defenses began to crumble under their assault; the Shadow Keepers were formidable but faltered under the relentless advance of light and shadow united. With each fallen Keeper, the path to Bellinor's twisted throne grew clearer.

But even as victory on this front seemed within grasp, Nadia knew this was but the first challenge they would face this night. The true test awaited within the heart of darkness itself, inside the Midnight Citadel.

Delving deeper into the heart of the Midnight Citadel, Nadia and Aidan navigated through its claustrophobic passages, the very essence of villainy thick in the atmosphere. The corridors wound before them, a maze devised by malevolence, its deceitful turns and blind alleys striving to disorient and trap its prey. Yet, the twins advanced with a sureness that defied the Citadel's treacherous design, driven by a connection to their destiny that drew them inexorably forward.

Wall sconces, emitting a ghastly green flame, were mounted in intervals along the corridor, throwing a sickening light that twisted the twins' shadows into monstrous shapes. Nadia, with each determined stride, stretched forth her hand, her gift of lightweaving slicing through the gloom. The once-ghoulish illumination transformed under her influence, metamorphosing into a beacon of pure, comforting light that washed over the corridor with a gentle warmth, as if the sun itself had descended to guide their way.

Beside her, Aidan's gift was the mirror to her own; a cool, enveloping presence. His shadow weaving surged forth, an invisible tide of darkness that was both shield and spear. It surged ahead of them, a silent guardian that quelled adversaries before they could brandish their weapons. Together, they orchestrated a dance of light and shadow, a union of opposing forces that left their overwhelmed foes staggering in disarray.

Faced with the Shadow Keepers, the twins encountered fleeting resistance, as those dark warriors converged, intent on halting their advance. Yet, where Nadia's radiant touch fell, it seemed to stir a flicker of confusion, a glimmer of some distant memory within the Keepers. Following this moment of vulnerability, Aidan's shadows would rise like a gentle tide, embracing them not with violence, but with a hushed offer of repose, lulling them into a deep and inescapable slumber.

Lysara moved like flowing water through the chaos, her silver-blue eyes shining as she wove light into barriers that shielded the advancing rebels. "This way!" she called to Nadia and Aidan, creating a path of light through the sea of shadows.

"Lysara!" Nadia shouted as a Shadow Keeper lunged at the lightweaver from behind.

Without turning, Lysara's hand flashed upward, a whip of light materializing to strike the attacker. "Stay focused on Bellinor," she instructed the twins. "This is your battle; the one you were born for. We'll handle the rest."

Nadia and Aidan stood before the imposing doors, grandiose and foreboding, their surfaces a tapestry of eternal nightfall; Bellinor's sanctum awaited them. With a silent communion that belied their bond, they pushed forth, the doors yielding to their resolve.

Before them, the throne room unfurled, a cavernous expanse that swallowed warmth and cheer. Colossal pillars stood sentinel along their path, their silent watch akin to that of ancient, stone behemoths. At the room's end, the throne of Queen Bellinor loomed; a construct not of regality but of palpable malevolence, a thing alive with its own ominous pulse.

The queen herself embodied majesty laced with dread. Her raven hair cascaded like a waterfall of shadow, laced with veins of silver that snared the meager light. Her gaze, sharp and cold as shards of frost, locked onto Nadia and Aidan, a chilling welcome into her domain of darkness.

Nadia and Aidan, united in purpose and power, faced the ominous figure of Queen Bellinor with unwavering determination. Her malevolent form towered before them, a stark contrast against the throne room's dim illumination, casting an oppressive pall over the grand space.

"You really think you can stand against me?" The Queen's voice slithered through the air, smooth as silk yet brimming with malice, its echo slinking along the stone walls.

"Such weak little lights, so easy to snuff out." Bellinor's voice cut through the air like ice, her words dripping with venom.

She circled them slowly, her cold eyes never leaving their faces. "Look at yourselves. Playing with powers you barely understand. Your parents couldn't stop me, and neither will you."

Aidan's face hardened. "We may be new to our powers," he shot back, "but we're the rightful heirs of Mirrathia. Together, we're going to end your reign of darkness."

Bellinor laughed, the sound hollow and chilling. "Let's see about that," she hissed, raising her hands as shadows coiled around her like serpents ready to strike.

Writhing shadows surged forth, taking the form of sinuous tendrils that aimed to ensnare and smother. But Nadia advanced, her hands emanating a searing luminance that sliced through the umbra, repelling the dark threats before they could graze their mortal coils.

Together, Aidan and Nadia embodied a harmony of contrasts, his own shadows rising in a protective dance to neutralize Bellinor's offensive. They were the embodiment of duality; light and darkness interwoven in a complex dance of supremacy.

The throne room transformed into a battleground of epic proportions, a contest of light against shadow. Queen Bellinor's dominion over darkness was formidable, as she conjured nefarious weapons; voracious swords and oppressive chains designed to ensnare the spirit.

But Nadia's light surged with every blow delivered by Bellinor, her brilliance forming impenetrable shields and fortifications, while Aidan's contravening shadows unfurled, meticulously dismantling Bellinor's dark creations with calculated precision.

In this royal chamber, the fates of the twins and Mirrathia hung in the balance, their collective wills and burgeoning powers colliding in a spectacular display that would forever shape the destiny of their world.

Bellinor's eyes narrowed as she assessed the twins. With a sudden flick of her wrists, shadows erupted from the floor, forming a wall that sliced between Nadia and Aidan, forcing them apart.

"You draw your strength from each other," she hissed, her voice like broken glass. "How touching. And how predictable."

The shadow wall solidified, stretching from floor to ceiling. Nadia slammed her fist against it, but her light couldn't penetrate its dense darkness. On the other side, she heard Aidan calling her name.

"Each of you alone is nothing," Bellinor said, circling Nadia like a predator. "Just like your parents."

The shadows around Bellinor began to shift and morph, rising from the floor and walls. They twisted into humanoid shapes with razor-sharp claws and empty eye sockets. The shadow creatures lurched forward, their movements jerky and unnatural.

"Hold on, Aidan!" Nadia shouted, hoping her brother could hear her through the barrier. She summoned her light, forming a glowing shield as the first shadow creature lunged.

Its claws screeched against her light, leaving trails of darkness that sizzled like acid. Nadia pushed back, her shield expanding in a burst that disintegrated the creature. But more were forming, their black bodies emerging from every corner of the throne room.

On the other side of the shadow wall, Aidan faced his own battle. Bellinor had left him to contend with a writhing mass of darkness that seemed alive, constantly shifting to counter his attacks. Every time he dissolved one section with his own shadows, it reformed elsewhere.

"You think you understand shadow?" Bellinor's voice echoed around him. "You're playing with forces beyond your comprehension."

A tendril of darkness shot out, wrapping around Aidan's ankle and yanking him off balance. He hit the floor hard, and immediately more tendrils snaked toward him. He rolled and slashed with a blade of shadow, cutting himself free.

"Nadia!" he called. "We need to break this barrier!"

Nadia heard her brother's voice, muffled but urgent. She was surrounded by shadow creatures now, fighting them off with increasingly desperate bursts of light. One slipped past her defenses, its claws raking across her shoulder. She cried out as pain lanced through her, hot and sharp.

Lysara's voice rang out from the entrance to the throne room. "Nadia, behind you!"

The lightweaver hurled a spear of concentrated light that impaled the shadow creature about to strike Nadia from behind. It dissolved with a shriek that seemed to vibrate the very air.

Lysara fought her way to Nadia's side, her movements fluid and precise. "The wall separating you," she said between attacks, "it's not just shadow, it's a manifestation of doubt. Your light can penetrate it if you believe."

Blood trickled down Nadia's arm from her wounded shoulder. "I can't get through," she gasped. "I've tried."

"Not alone," Lysara said, deflecting another shadow creature. "Focus on your connection to Aidan. Feel it. Trust it."

Nadia closed her eyes for a split second, centering herself amid the chaos. She reached out with her senses, feeling for that thread that had always connected her to Aidan, even when she hadn't known he existed.

There... a pulse, a resonance that felt like looking in a mirror and seeing a familiar face. She channeled her light toward it, not attacking the wall but seeking the presence on the other side.

On his side, Aidan felt the warmth of Nadia's light calling to him. He pressed his hand against the shadow barrier, his own power responding to hers. Where they connected, a pinpoint of brilliance formed, growing larger as their powers synchronized.

Bellinor saw what was happening and snarled. She abandoned her attack on Aidan and rushed toward the weakening barrier, hands outstretched and trailing darkness like smoke.

"Lysara, now!" Captain Grey shouted from the doorway, where he and a squad of rebels had been fighting to reach the throne room.

Lysara gathered her strength and hurled a blinding flash of light directly at Bellinor. The queen shrieked as the radiance struck her, momentarily halting her advance.

In that crucial moment, the point of light where Nadia and Aidan's powers met exploded outward. The shadow wall shattered like glass, fragments of darkness dissolving into nothing.

Nadia stumbled forward, clutching her injured shoulder. Aidan rushed to her side, supporting her with one arm.

"You're hurt," he said, face etched with concern.

"I'm fine," she replied, though her voice was tight with pain. "We need to finish this."

Bellinor recovered quickly, her rage palpable as she gathered the remaining shadows to her. They swirled around her like a tempest, growing denser and darker until she seemed to be standing at the center of a miniature storm.

"You think your little family reunion changes anything?" she spat. "I've ruled Mirrathia for years. Your parents couldn't stop me. No one can!"

"We're not our parents," Aidan said.

"We're something new," Nadia added.

They stood side by side, their shoulders touching. Despite Nadia's injury, her light flared brighter than ever, feeding off Aidan's presence. His shadows grew more defined, more controlled, shaped by her clarity.

Together, they reached out, light and shadow extending from their fingertips like two halves of the same spell. Where the powers met, they didn't cancel each other out but merged, creating something neither had seen before; a force that was neither light nor shadow but something transcendent.

Bellinor's eyes widened as she realized what was happening. She backed away, her shadow storm faltering as she glanced over her shoulder, searching for escape.

The twins advanced step by step, their combined power growing with each movement. It spiraled around them in a double helix of radiance and darkness, humming with energy that made the air itself vibrate.

"This ends now," they said in unison, their voices harmonizing as perfectly as their powers.

With a synchronized thrust of their hands, they released the full force of their combined might. It surged forward like a tidal wave, overwhelming everything in its path. Bellinor tried to counter with her shadows, but they were swept away like cobwebs before a gale.

The wave struck Bellinor and the throne behind her, the impact creating a deafening boom that shook the entire citadel. The force of it threw Nadia and Aidan backward, sending them tumbling across the floor.

When they looked up, dazed from the impact, the throne was in ruins; a pile of broken stone and twisted metal. Of Bellinor, there was no sign except a scorch mark on the floor and something small glinting in the center of it.

The twins pushed themselves to their feet, supporting each other as they approached the spot where Bellinor had stood. There, half-hidden among the debris, lay a small hand mirror, its surface dark and still.

Lysara joined them, her expression grave as she looked down at the mirror.

"Is she..." Nadia began.

"Gone," Lysara finished, though something in her tone suggested uncertainty. "Like the other Shadow Keepers you faced."

Aidan knelt to examine the mirror but didn't touch it. "What's this doing here?"

Lysara shook her head. "A remnant of her power, perhaps.

Shadow Keepers often carried objects to amplify their abilities."

The rebels flooded into the throne room, cheers rising as they saw the destroyed throne and the twins standing victorious. Captain Grey approached, his weathered face breaking into a rare smile.

"It's over," he said, surveying the scene. "You've done it."

As the celebration erupted around them, Nadia and Aidan exchanged a glance. Something felt unfinished, a question without an answer. But for now, they allowed themselves to be swept up in the moment, in the joy of their people and the knowledge that they had, at least for today, brought light back to Mirrathia.

In the midst of the revelry, no one noticed as a rebel accidentally kicked the small mirror, sending it spinning across the floor until it came to rest against a wall, its surface briefly rippling like disturbed water before going still again.

The rebels gathered at the chamber's edge watched with bated breath, uncertain of what victory might look like. The air itself seemed suspended, caught between darkness and dawn.

Then, as if responding to an ancient call woven into the very stones, the Midnight Citadel began to transform. The shadows that had clung like parasites to every surface for years began to recoil and retreat. They peeled away like mist before sunlight, revealing beneath them not the scorched ruins one might expect, but surfaces that gleamed with an inner radiance.

One by one, the twisted sconces that had held sickly green flames now burst with golden light, each torch igniting in a wave that spread outward from the throne room. The cold that had permeated these halls for so long gave way to a gentle warmth that seemed to breathe life back into the stone itself.

Outside, the jagged spires that had once resembled fangs against the sky softened their edges. The obsidian towers that had been warped by malice straightened, their surfaces brightening from black to shimmering ivory that caught the sunlight and reflected it in prismatic brilliance. Windows that had been opaque with shadow cleared like ice melting, allowing sunlight to pour through in colorful beams where once only darkness had reigned.

The rebels' gazes tracked each transformation with awestruck wonder. The ceiling, which had hung low and oppressive with stalactites of shadow, now soared upward in graceful arches. Frescoes long hidden beneath layers of darkness revealed themselves; scenes of Mirrathia's golden age, of families celebrating under open skies, of harmony between light and shadow in perfect balance.

Where the marble floors had been cracked and stained with what looked unsettlingly like dried blood, they now knit themselves together, the surface polished to a mirror sheen that reflected the light from above. The walls, which had exuded a sense of watchfulness and malice, now seemed to stand protective and welcoming, their carvings depicting stories of wisdom and courage rather than conquest and subjugation.

Most striking of all was the transformation of the throne room itself. The raised dais where Bellinor's twisted throne had dominated now lay empty, a circular platform bathed in sunlight streaming through a newly formed oculus in the ceiling. The black metal and jagged stone of her seat had dissolved completely, leaving no trace that it had ever existed.

In its place stood nothing but possibility; an empty circle waiting to be filled with new purpose and hope. The very air within the chamber, which had once felt thick and suffocating, now moved freely, carrying the scent of spring blossoms that had no business blooming inside a castle.

As the Palace of Light reclaimed its true nature, shedding the corruption of Bellinor's reign like a snake casting off old skin, even the most battle-hardened rebels felt tears spring to their eyes. Some fell to their knees, overcome by the beauty of what they were witnessing. Others laughed in disbelief, the sound of joy echoing in chambers that had known only fear for too long.

Captain Grey stood amidst his warriors, his scarred face upturned to watch as crystal chandeliers that had hung like stalactites of ice now refracted light in dancing patterns across the walls. "By all the light," he whispered, "I never thought I'd live to see this day."

Lysara moved through the transformed space, her fingers trailing along walls that now responded to her touch with subtle pulses of light. "The palace remembers," she said, her voice filled with wonder. "It remembers what it was meant to be."

Nadia and Aidan stood at the center of it all, their hands still clasped together, both exhausted yet exhilarated by what they had accomplished. Around them, the Palace of Light continued its metamorphosis, each moment revealing new wonders as centuries of darkness were undone by the power of their combined heritage.

The rebellion had dreamed of victory, but none had dared imagine something as complete as this; not just the defeat of an enemy, but the restoration of a legacy they had known only in stories. As the celebrations began in earnest around them, the twins exchanged a glance that spoke volumes. They had reclaimed their birthright, but the journey was far from over.

And somewhere in the shadows that retreated to the deepest corners of the palace, something stirred; a darkness that had survived, waiting and watching. A wisp of malice that slithered between cracks in the foundation, silent as a secret and just as potent.

CHAPTER TEN: A RIFT BETWEEN ROYALS

The Palace of Light, once a hollow echo of its name, thrummed with the renewed vigor of a hive in spring. Its walls, cleansed of the shadow that had once clung to them like a blight, now resonated with the hammering of nails, the chime of silverware, and the swish of brooms as servants, both old and new, tended to their duties with a zeal born of newfound hope.

In the throne room, where light from the high windows danced upon the marble floor, artisans and carpenters labored side by side. Their task was to create not one, but two thrones worthy of the twin heirs who had brought dawn back to their dusk-veiled land. Craftsmen consulted faded tapestries for guidance, seeking to honor tradition while embracing the fresh start that Nadia and Aidan's reign promised.

Where there had been but a single chair, grand in its solitude, a pair now rose. Twin thrones carved from ethereal wood that mirrored each other in design yet bore unique flourishes; a testament to the individuality of each sovereign-to-be. The carvers worked with loving care, etching symbols of light and shadow into the armrests, intertwining their fates just as their destinies were bound together.

In quieter chambers, jewelers hunched over workbenches strewn with tools and gemstones. Crowns were taking shape beneath their skilled hands: delicate circlets destined to rest upon royal brows. They wove gold and silver into intricate patterns, setting sapphires and emeralds into metal with tender taps. Each stone was chosen for its luster and depth, imbued with the essence of Mirrathia itself.

Elsewhere in the palace, seamstresses measured and cut fine cloth for the ceremonial garb. The fabrics, silk and velvet, whispered secrets of ancient looms as they fell in elegant folds around mannequins. The colors chosen were those of dawn and twilight: soft pinks and purples mingling with hues of vibrant green and blue.

Outside, heralds practiced their proclamations, their voices rising and falling in melodious cadence as they perfected every intonation for the ceremony ahead. Gardeners trimmed hedges into shapes befitting royalty while florists threaded blooms into garlands to festoon halls and archways.

As the sun dipped toward the horizon, casting long shadows across bustling courtyards and busy halls alike, there was a sense among all that this was not just preparation for a coronation; it was the weaving together of a kingdom's fragmented heartstrings into a melody of unity and strength.

Amidst the jubilant echoes in the Palace of Light, a hush descended as the moment of coronation approached. The once shadow-veiled hall now shimmered with luminous streams, reflecting off polished marble and glinting metals. Garin, in his ceremonial garb adorned with symbols of ancient guardianship, stepped forward bearing the crowns; a twin set of delicate silver and radiant gemstones, forged from Mirrathia's own heart.

The throne room, now bathed in the gentle glow of the restored Palace of Light, thrummed with the joyous clamor of a realm reborn. The rebels, once clad in the drab hues of secrecy and battle, now adorned themselves with vibrant colors that mirrored the radiance around them. In every corner, the air was thick with laughter and song, a chorus of freedom that had been muted for far too long.

Nadia and Aidan stood at the heart of it all, their presence like twin beacons drawing eyes and hearts alike. There were no crowns upon their heads this day, no scepters in their hands. Instead, they were enfolded by the love and gratitude of their people; a mantle more profound than any regalia.

Clara moved through the throng with grace, her hands weaving strands of light into garlands that fluttered to rest upon shoulders and wrists; bonds of unity for all to bear. She approached Nadia and Aidan with a smile that rivaled the warmth surrounding them.

"These are for you," she said, draping a loop of glowing flowers around each of their necks. "They are simple but carry our essence; our life force intertwined."

Nadia touched the petals gently, feeling their light pulse against her skin in time with her heartbeat. "Thank you," she said, her voice thick with emotion.

Aidan glanced around at the faces alight with happiness and determination. "We rebuild together," he affirmed. "Every stone placed in hope, every path cleared in solidarity."

Elan bounded up to them with his irrepressible grin, his eyes sparkling as much as the ale in his cup. "Let's not forget to enjoy ourselves! We've earned this moment!"

Laughter rippled through those gathered as they took Elan's words to heart. With each passing moment, joy wove itself into the fabric of Mirrathia anew; a tapestry rich with tales yet to be told.

Aidan stood tall, his gaze steady and filled with the gravity of the mantle he was about to assume. Beside him, Nadia's eyes gleamed with a mix of resolve and wonder, her journey from the girl who once felt out of place to a queen now rooted in purpose.

Lysara, her hair flowing like woven strands of moonlight, moved to stand before them. She held the crowns aloft for all to see, her voice clear as she spoke the words of ascension. "In the light of truth and the warmth of hope, we crown you Aidan and Nadia, sovereigns of Mirrathia."

With practiced grace, she placed the crown upon Aidan's head first. It settled with a weight that was more than physical; it was the weight of legacy, of futures yet unwritten. Next came Nadia's turn, and as the crown touched her brow, it was as if the very light within her found its home.

Together they turned to face their people from their thrones; two halves of a whole reunited. The assembly erupted in cheers that filled every corner of the palace, spilling into the streets of Avaloria where citizens gathered to share in this historic moment.

Banners unfurled from balconies, their vibrant hues catching the sunlight that now streamed unimpeded through city and countryside alike. Children ran through open plazas with ribbons and laughter trailing behind them like comet tails.

At long last, peace settled upon Mirrathia like a gentle cloak. The coronation feast commenced; a spread rich with flavors from every corner of the realm. Music swelled in joyous melodies while dancers spun in celebration of light's return.

Garin stepped forward, his weathered face etched with pride as he addressed the assembly. "Friends, warriors of light, we stand united not just by our struggle, but by our hope. Today marks not an end but a beginning... the dawn of Mirrathia's new age under its rightful heirs."

Applause erupted like a wave crashing against the shore, resounding through the hall. Captain Grey raised his cup high, his gruff voice carrying over the din. "To Nadia and Aidan! May their reign be long and their light never falter!"

"To Nadia and Aidan!" The crowd echoed, their voices a harmonious swell that filled every inch of space.

The rebels mingled with nobles and common folk alike, each

story intertwined, each fate reclaimed from darkness' grip. And there at the center were Aidan and Nadia, their smiles reflecting a kingdom reborn.

As the last echoes of celebration dimmed to a warm, murmuring hum, Aidan and Nadia stood before their subjects, their hands joined in solidarity. The crowd hushed, a collective breath held in anticipation of the twins' first decree as sovereigns.

Aidan's voice resonated through the hall, steady and reassuring. "People of Mirrathia, today marks not just the end of tyranny but the dawn of our shared future. We stand before you as your servants, committed to mending the fractures that have scarred our realm."

Nadia's voice followed, harmonizing with her brother's resolve. "We vow to rebuild what was lost, to heal wounds both seen and hidden. Our path will be one of restoration and unity. This is our solemn promise to you."

Murmurs of approval rose from the gathered crowd, a wave of hopeful whispers that promised collaboration and renewal.

Aidan's gaze swept across the familiar faces in the throng; warriors who had become friends, citizens who had borne too much. "To guide us on this path, we will need wisdom and strength by our side."

Nadia nodded, her expression resolute as she continued their pledge. "That is why we appoint Garin and Captain Grey as our trusted advisors. With their counsel, we will forge a kingdom where light prevails and darkness has no dominion."

Garin stepped forward, his weathered face softening with pride.

He bowed deeply before the twins. "Your Majesties, I am honored to serve Mirrathia once more, under your fair and just rule."

Lastly came Captain Grey, his scars a testament to his unwavering dedication to Mirrathia's freedom. He saluted crisply; a warrior's vow etched into the gesture. "You have my sword and my loyalty," he declared. "Together, we shall rise from the ashes of Bellinor's reign."

The assembly burst into applause; a thunderous affirmation of unity and hope for what lay ahead under the rule of Aidan and Nadia.

Amidst the jubilant echoes in the Palace of Light, a hush descended as Talia approached the twins, her expression somber, her eyes reflecting a storm that had not yet passed. She moved with deliberate grace, her presence a gentle counterbalance to the exuberance that permeated the air.

"Nadia, Aidan," she spoke, her voice low but clear, cutting through the sound of hammers and saws like a knife through silk. "A moment, if you will."

The twins exchanged a glance before following Talia to a quiet alcove where the sounds of reconstruction faded to a distant hum. Sunlight streamed through newly restored stained glass, casting jewel-toned patterns across their faces.

"The deed is done," Talia began, her hands clasped before her, "and Bellinor's reign has ended. But..." She paused, her gaze drifting to the shadows that still lingered in the corners of the palace.

Aidan straightened, his posture alert. "But what, Talia?"

"Her physical form may be no more; a triumph, indeed," Talia said, choosing her words with care. "Yet within the remnants of darkness that flee from this place, I sense... something unfinished."

Nadia's hand found Aidan's, their fingers intertwining in an instinctive gesture of unity. "What do you mean?" she asked, her voice barely above a whisper.

"An essence lingers," Talia explained, her eyes narrowing as if trying to perceive something just beyond sight. "It's elusive, a wisp of darkness that evades even my sight. Bellinor was deeply entrenched in the dark arts; it is possible that a fragment of her malice survives."

Nadia felt a chill snake down her spine despite the warmth of the sun-drenched alcove. "Can it be stopped? Banished for good?"

Talia shook her head slowly, silver hair catching the light. "Some shadows are bound to this realm in ways we may not fully comprehend."

"Then we'll remain vigilant," Aidan declared, his jaw set with determination. "We'll guard against her return—no matter what form it may take."

Talia placed a hand on each of their shoulders; a seer's touch that was both comforting and imbued with the gravity of their shared destiny. "You have brought light back to Mirrathia," she affirmed. "And as long as that light burns within you both, darkness will find no purchase here."

As Talia withdrew, leaving them to consider her words, a figure appeared at the edge of the throne room; an elderly man with silver hair and sharp, calculating eyes that missed nothing as they surveyed the transformation taking place. His robes, once black and silver in Bellinor's court, had been hastily redyed in shades of blue and gold;

the traditional colors of royal advisors.

"Your Majesties," he called, approaching with a deep bow that seemed practiced to perfection. "I am Councilor Gerald Rathbone. I come to pledge my loyalty, as I once served your esteemed parents, King Alaric and Queen Valora."

A wave of murmurs, laced with suspicion and covert glances, rippled through the crowd as they pondered the weight of Rathbone's avowal, with many reflecting on his conspicuous absence during the realm's darkest hours.

Nadia felt something stir within her—a wariness that tightened her shoulders and set her teeth on edge. Beside her, Aidan stepped forward, his expression curious rather than cautious.

"Councilor Rathbone," Aidan replied, his voice carrying the weight of his newfound authority. "Your presence is unexpected but welcome. We have much to learn about our parents' reign."

As Rathbone smiled—a gesture that didn't quite reach his eyes—Nadia couldn't help but wonder if this was part of what Talia had sensed. Not Bellinor herself, perhaps, but something of her influence persisting in those who had served her. She glanced toward the alcove where Talia had been, but the seer had vanished, leaving only dappled light where she had stood.

Suspicion lingered in the air, as tangible as the cool night breeze that swept through the throng of onlookers. Captain Grey moved closer to the twins, his eyes locked on Rathbone with unspoken wariness.

"Your intelligence could indeed prove useful," Grey conceded with reluctant practicality. "However, trust is not so easily granted." His gaze turned to Aidan and Nadia. "We must exercise caution with those who have walked in shadows."

Nadia felt Aidan's hand on her shoulder, a silent reminder of their shared responsibility to discern truth from deceit. The whispers of the crowd grew louder, a chorus of doubt and curiosity intermingling in the night air.

Rathbone bowed slightly, acknowledging Captain Grey's words. "Skepticism serves you well," he affirmed. "Allow me to prove my loyalty through action rather than mere oaths."

Amidst this charged atmosphere, Garin, a living archive of forgotten lore, advanced, his countenance etched with contemplation. His penetrating stare assessed Rathbone's unexpected return. Although skepticism cast its shadow, Garin's response was suffused with the assurance only experience can bestow. "Allegiance to the crown of old holds no trifling place. In bygone eras, his constancy was the backbone of our sovereignty's inner sanctum."

The twins shared a glance brimming with unspoken thoughts, their expressions a tapestry of caution woven with an intense yearning for the truth. The enigmatic circumstances of Rathbone's return, while veiled in mystery, teased the possibility of unraveling ancestral secrets entwined with the very core of their heritage.

Rathbone's pledge, while grand in gesture, left an uneasy chill in the air, a subtle dissonance amidst the celebration's warmth. He bowed deeply before the twin rulers, his eyes gleaming with an intensity that belied his grandfatherly facade.

"Your Majesties," he began, his voice a smooth timbre of feigned humility, "I offer you not just my allegiance but the wisdom and experience garnered from my years of service under your esteemed parents. In these times of change, guidance is a treasure more precious than the rarest of jewels."

Nadia watched Rathbone with a cautious eye. His words flowed like honey, sweet and practiced, yet she couldn't shake the feeling that beneath that sweet exterior lay something bitter. She had learned to trust her instincts; they had kept her alive in this strange world thus far.

Aidan accepted Rathbone's words with a gracious nod. "We thank you for your offer, Councilor. Your counsel will be invaluable as we navigate the path of rulership." His voice resonated with the confidence of a born leader, yet it carried no trace of naivety. He too felt the weight of Rathbone's presence, a burden cloaked in silken words.

As the crowd dispersed to continue their revelries, Nadia leaned close to Aidan. Her voice was a whisper meant only for her brother's ears. "There's something about Rathbone... A shadow that doesn't match the light he's trying to cast."

Aidan met her gaze, his own apprehension mirroring hers. "We'll keep him close," he replied. "If there are secrets hidden within him, we'll draw them out in due time." His expression hardened with resolve, yet it did nothing to dispel the unease that had settled in Nadia's chest.

They parted from Rathbone with courteous farewells and

promises to confer on matters of state at dawn. As they moved through the throngs of their people, Nadia remained vigilant. Rathbone had pledged his allegiance, but she would not let his honeyed words cloud her judgment nor dim the light they fought so hard to restore.

Aidan led the way to the once-great hall of the Palace of Light, now bustling with the energy of rebirth. Workers scurried about, mending tapestries and polishing the age-worn marble. In the midst of this renewal, Rathbone followed, his gaze sweeping across the chamber with an air of proprietary nostalgia.

The twins settled at a grand table, maps and scrolls unfurled before them. The kingdom was in tatters; its people scattered and its resources plundered. Rebuilding Mirrathia would be no simple feat.

Rathbone pulled a chair up to the table, rolling out a parchment that detailed the administrative divisions of the kingdom. "Your parents had a vision for this land," he began, his finger tracing the borders of long-forgotten provinces. "Unity through strength and prosperity through knowledge."

Aidan listened intently, soaking in Rathbone's every word. "We must reconnect with the outlying villages first," he decided, pointing to a cluster of dots representing hamlets nestled in the valleys. "They've been isolated for too long."

Nadia nodded in agreement but remained silent, her thoughts on Rathbone's silver-tongued assurances. She kept her skepticism hidden beneath a mask of concentration as she perused another scroll.

The challenges were many; roads needed repair to ensure safe travel, farms required restoration to prevent famine, and local militias had to be disarmed or integrated into a national defense force.

As they discussed these issues, Rathbone interjected with insights and historical precedents. "Your father often spoke of 'The Chain of Prosperity,'" he reminisced. "Each link, food, safety, education, must be strong for Mirrathia to thrive."

Aidan absorbed this philosophy with a keen interest. Here was knowledge from an era when Mirrathia was whole; a time before darkness crept over their lands.

The sun dipped low in the sky as they labored over plans and policies. Aidan could feel the weight of their task but found strength in Rathbone's presence; a connection to his parents he never knew he yearned for.

As dusk turned to nightfall, Nadia observed her brother's interactions with Rathbone from across the table. She trusted Aidan's judgment but couldn't help but wonder if their newfound advisor held secrets beneath his helpful exterior. Nevertheless, she focused on her work, knowing that only through unity could they face the monumental task ahead.

As the moon rose, casting its pale light through the tall windows of the palace, Nadia's disquiet grew. Rathbone's every word seemed laced with a double meaning, his every gesture too calculated. The sense of unease coiled in her stomach like a snake.

Aidan, buoyed by the sense of connection to their parents' legacy, failed to notice Nadia's discomfort. "He knows so much, Nadia," Aidan said one evening as they walked through the dimly lit corridors of the palace. "Rathbone's guidance has been invaluable."

Nadia hesitated, her gaze flickering to Rathbone, who trailed a few steps behind, hands clasped behind his back. "I don't doubt his knowledge," she replied carefully, "but something about him just doesn't sit right with me."

Aidan frowned, the first signs of a rift forming between them. "We need all the help we can get," he said, his tone more clipped than he intended. "You can't let baseless suspicions divide us."

Nadia wanted to argue, to tell Aidan that her instincts were rarely wrong, but she held her tongue. Instead, she forced a smile and nodded, letting the matter drop for the moment.

Outside the palace walls, the people of Mirrathia faced their own turmoil. Despite their joy at Bellinor's defeat and their reverence for the twins' heroics, uncertainty gnawed at their hearts.

In market squares and taverns, whispers spread about what changes the new rulership would bring. The common folk traded stories of their encounters with Bellinor's dark reign; each tale a mix of sorrow and hope.

Farmers deliberated over whether the harvest would be bountiful under Nadia and Aidan's rule or if famine would continue to grip their lands. Merchants wondered if trade routes would reopen and if prosperity would return.

Parents tucked their children into bed with stories of a brighter future while silently questioning what role they would play in this new chapter of Mirrathia.

The weight of expectation hung heavy in the air as Nadia and Aidan stepped into roles they were never prepared for; rulers of a fractured kingdom seeking the light after an age of darkness.

Day by day, Nadia and Aidan immersed themselves in the governance of Mirrathia, their resolve as unyielding as the stone walls of the palace. They met with farmers and merchants, listened to the woes of the common folk, and drafted decrees that aimed to heal the wounds of their land.

Aidan's voice rang clear in the great hall, filled with subjects seeking guidance. "We will establish caravans to distribute food to those most affected by the famine," he declared, his green eyes reflecting the determination that fueled his spirit.

Nadia stood by his side, her presence a beacon of hope. "And we shall rebuild," she added, her gaze sweeping across the faces before her. "Not just homes and markets, but trust and unity."

Yet as they worked to sew the seeds of a new era, shadows lingered in forgotten corners of Mirrathia. At dusk, when the sun dipped below the horizon, a chill crept through the streets, and people hurried home with anxious glances over their shoulders.

As the fledgling rulers of Mirrathia, Nadia and Aidan navigated the complexities of their newfound responsibilities with youthful zeal. Their days brimmed with audiences and councils, the voices of their people shaping the dawn of their reign.

One morning, as a rosy glow suffused the throne room, Rathbone approached the twins with a meticulously crafted suggestion. "Your Highnesses," he began, his voice a melodic cadence of concern and respect. "I've pondered upon our agricultural plight and propose we import grain from the Eastern Valleys."

Aidan leaned forward, his fingers steepled in contemplation. "But isn't that land treacherous, riddled with remnants of Bellinor's influence?"

Rathbone's eyes glinted with a calculated innocence. "True, yet the harvest there is bountiful. A little risk could yield great reward for our people."

Nadia shifted uneasily in her seat, her instincts prickling with disquiet. "And what of our own farmers? They need support to recover from the darkness that blighted their crops."

Rathbone offered a placating smile. "Indeed, Princess Nadia. Yet recovery takes time, and our people hunger now. This measure would merely be... temporary."

"That's Queen, Councilor," reminded Nadia.

"My apologies, Your Majesty."

Aidan nodded slowly, considering Rathbone's words as he often did. The older man's advice carried weight born of experience; a guiding hand in a world still strange to the young rulers.

As Rathbone retreated with a bow, leaving his proposal hanging like ripe fruit in the minds of the twins, Nadia felt a ripple of unease that she couldn't quite place.

The twins convened later in private council, Aidan pacing before an ancient tapestry depicting Mirrathia's lush landscapes. "Rathbone may have a point," he mused aloud.

Nadia wrapped her arms around herself, a chill settling in her bones despite the warmth of spring air wafting through open windows. "There's something... off about this," she murmured more to herself than to Aidan.

"Perhaps," Aidan conceded with a sigh. "But we must act swiftly. Our people can't wait for maybes and feelings."

And so it was decided. Messengers were dispatched to negotiate passage through the Eastern Valleys; an uneasy alliance forged on Rathbone's subtle urging.

In the days that followed, wagons laden with grain wound their way toward Avaloria, while whispers of unease stirred among those who worked the land; those who knew every furrow and seed sown by their hands.

In the stillness of her chambers, Talia gazed into a basin of water that shimmered with an ethereal light. Her brow furrowed as murky shapes twisted within its depths; a darkness that defied her sight.

She turned away from her scrying tools with a sigh. Though Bellinor's reign had ended, Talia knew that shadows did not yield so easily. Her visions were clouded with whispers and echoes of malice that refused to be silenced.

In the privacy of her study, she confided in Garin. "The shadow has not lifted completely," she murmured, her fingers tracing lines of worry on her brow.

Garin's hand found hers, his touch grounding. "We've faced darkness before," he said. "We'll face it again... together."

Talia nodded, drawing strength from his unwavering support. But in her heart, uncertainty reigned. The dark presence was elusive, always just beyond her reach; a puzzle that demanded to be solved for Mirrathia's future to be truly secure.

The council chamber, usually a place of unity and decision, brimmed with an undercurrent of discord that evening. Tapestries along the walls bore silent witness to the rising tensions between the twin rulers of Mirrathia. Nadia sat rigid, her every muscle coiled like a spring as Rathbone laid out his latest plans for the realm's defense.

Aidan, who had been nodding along to Rathbone's words, failed to notice the storm brewing in his sister's eyes until she interrupted.

"You see threats in every shadow," Nadia snapped, her voice echoing against the stone walls. "But it's your counsel that sows seeds of doubt and fear."

The room fell silent. All eyes turned to Nadia, whose fingers gripped the armrests of her throne, knuckles whitening.

Rathbone's lips curled into a semblance of a reassuring smile. "Your Highness," he began, his tone soothing, "prudence is not the enemy. It is our shield against..."

"It is control you seek," Nadia cut him off sharply. "You weave words like a spider spins webs, catching those who listen in strands of manipulation."

Aidan rose to his feet, frustration etched into his features.

"Enough!" His voice boomed louder than he intended, bouncing off the chamber walls. "Rathbone has been nothing but loyal since he joined our court."

Nadia stood to face him directly, her green eyes aflame with a passion that matched her brother's intensity. "How can you not see it? He's playing us for fools; guiding your hand while you hold the scepter."

Aidan's fists clenched at his sides. "Your accusations are baseless!" His chest heaved with each breath as he fought to maintain composure.

"Is it so baseless to question? To fear that our parents' old ally might still harbor loyalties to their usurper?" Nadia's words cut through the air, sharp and clear.

Rathbone observed the exchange, his expression unreadable, yet there was no mistaking the glint in his eye; a spark that might have been triumph or amusement.

"I trust Rathbone," Aidan declared. "Your paranoia serves no one; not you, not me, and certainly not Mirrathia."

Nadia recoiled as if struck. The rift between them yawned wider with each uttered word; a chasm neither sibling knew how to bridge.

Under the silver glow of the moon, Nadia paced the length of her chamber, the hem of her gown whispering against the cold stone floor. Each step was a silent echo of the unrest that knotted her insides. Her thoughts swirled like leaves caught in an autumn gale, each one a flicker of doubt about Rathbone.

The door creaked open, and Clara stepped inside, her presence a gentle tide washing over the shores of Nadia's troubled mind. The healer's eyes, warm and knowing, settled on the young queen with a softness that invited trust.

"Nadia," Clara began, her voice as soothing as the lullabies she once sang to wounded rebels. "You've summoned me at a late hour. What burdens your heart?"

Nadia halted her pacing and faced Clara. In those verdant eyes, a storm brewed; a tempest born of intuition and unease.

"It's Rathbone," Nadia confessed, the words tumbling out like river stones. "Something about him unsettles me."

Clara listened intently, her gaze never wavering from Nadia's face.

"I see his loyalty, his eagerness to serve," Nadia continued, wringing her hands together. "But beneath his smiles and nods, there's a shadow I can't ignore."

Before Clara could respond, another figure appeared in the doorway... Garin, his brow creased with concern.

"You called for me as well?" Garin inquired, stepping into the room. His eyes moved from Clara to Nadia, piecing together the silent story etched on their faces.

Nadia nodded, drawing a deep breath as she gathered her resolve. "Yes. I fear Rathbone may not be the ally he claims to be."

Garin crossed the room in three measured strides, his stance protective as he neared Nadia. "Speak your mind," he urged gently.

Nadia met Garin's steady gaze and found herself anchored by it.

She spoke of Rathbone's grandfatherly facade, of conversations overheard and glances that lingered too long.

"I can't shake this feeling," she admitted. "His counsel often leads us down strange paths; diversions that benefit no one but himself."

Clara and Garin exchanged a look; a silent conversation between two souls who had weathered countless storms together.

"We will keep watch," Garin assured Nadia, his voice firm with conviction. "And if Rathbone is weaving deception among us, we shall unravel it thread by thread."

With Clara at her side and Garin's unwavering support, Nadia felt a weight lift from her shoulders. Together they would face whatever challenges Rathbone might bring... and they would do so with eyes wide open.

CHAPTER ELEVEN: THE UNBREAKABLE BOND

Avaloria awoke like a slumbering giant, its streets stretching and buildings standing tall as the first rays of dawn kissed the rooftops. The city, once veiled in Bellinor's shadowy grasp, now shimmered with a renewed vigor as light returned to every corner and crevice.

The marketplace of Radiant Square buzzed with activity, merchants throwing open their shutters to let the light flood their stores. The vibrant colors of their awnings, once dulled by the oppressive darkness, now blazed beneath the sun in brilliant reds, blues, and golds. Children's laughter, a sound long muffled by fear and uncertainty, mingled with the calls of vendors hawking their goods.

Celestial Heights, where despair had once hung heavy in the air, thrived anew. The manors gleamed with fresh paint and repaired stonework, their gardens blossoming with flowers that reached for the sky in a defiant display of beauty. The noble district's grandeur stood restored, a testament to Mirrathia's resilience.

The River of Reflections flowed with newfound clarity, its waters mirroring the rejuvenated cityscape. The delicate bridges that spanned its breadth now served as meeting places for friends and lovers reunited in joy after the long darkness. At night, lanterns lit the riverbanks once more, creating a dance of flickering lights upon the water's surface.

At the heart of Avaloria's rebirth was the Palace of Light. Workers swarmed its halls like bees in a hive, repairing damage inflicted during Bellinor's reign. The palace's ivory towers shone bright against the azure backdrop of the sky; a beacon of hope for all who looked upon it.

The Luminous Library saw scholars returning to its vast halls with fervor. Knowledge that had been hidden away for protection against Bellinor's prying eyes resurfaced; ancient tomes and scrolls laid out on tables as eager minds set about reclaiming their cultural heritage.

As Nadia and Aidan walked through Avaloria's streets, they witnessed firsthand the fruits of their victory. Each smile from a passerby, each gleeful shout from a child playing in the square was a confirmation that their struggle had not been in vain.

Yet it was not just physical restoration that marked Avaloria's revival but an awakening spirit within its people; a collective determination to never again allow darkness to extinguish their light.

Amidst the sounds of hammers clinking and stone scraping against stone, Nadia and Aidan surveyed the restoration of Avaloria with a sense of pride. They moved through the streets, their presence a reassuring sight to the workers who toiled under the warm sun, rebuilding what had been lost.

Garin and their new advisor Rathbone flanked the twins, offering counsel on matters from resource allocation to preserving historical landmarks. The advisors' wisdom was invaluable, yet as Avaloria's renewal progressed, the twins found their own views diverging.

Aidan leaned heavily on Rathbone's experience, nodding thoughtfully at his suggestions for restructuring the city guard. "Rathbone's right," Aidan said. "A stronger defense force will ensure we're never caught off guard again."

Nadia hesitated, her gaze lingering on a group of children chasing each other around a newly erected fountain. "But we can't let fear dictate our future. Our people need hope, not just walls and weapons." Her words carried softly but firmly to her brother.

Rathbone gave Nadia a placating smile. "Of course, Your Highness, but we must not neglect our defenses. Balance is key."

Garin stepped in with a supportive nod toward Nadia. "The Queen has a point. Our focus should also be on healing and education. Strength isn't solely martial."

Nadia chimed in, her voice steady and sure. "Rebuilding isn't just about bricks and mortar; it's about community and trust."

The twins turned toward each other, green eyes meeting in silent conversation. They both knew that leading together meant compromise; a dance they were still learning the steps to.

As they continued their walk through the bustling marketplace, a dispute arose over trade agreements with neighboring realms. Rathbone pushed for exclusive contracts favoring Mirrathia's wealthier merchants.

Aidan considered the proposal with interest. "It would certainly boost our economy quickly," he mused.

Nadia furrowed her brows in concern. "But what of the smaller traders? They've suffered too. Shouldn't our policies ensure that all have an equal chance to recover?"

The tension between them was palpable as they stood amidst the chatter of bartering merchants and clinking coins, a stark contrast to their shared harmony in battle.

In every decision they faced, it seemed their unity frayed slightly at the edges; Nadia driven by empathy and inclusivity, Aidan by pragmatism and strength. Their advisors watched on with mixed expressions as Mirrathia's monarchs grappled with governance's delicate balance.

In the weeks that followed, Rathbone's influence within the royal circle grew, his counsel seemingly indispensable to Aidan. Yet with each strategic session and late-night discussion, Nadia's unease deepened like the shadows at dusk.

One afternoon, as the golden light of the setting sun painted

Avaloria's walls in hues of amber and rose, Nadia observed Rathbone from a balcony overlooking the training yard. He stood beside Aidan, gesturing towards the guards with a commanding presence that belied his grandfatherly appearance.

Aidan watched Rathbone with admiration, nodding along to his every word. "His experience is invaluable," Aidan had said time and again, and while Nadia couldn't dispute Rathbone's knowledge of court intricacies and military strategy, she couldn't shake the feeling that Rathbone's smiles were too calculated, his eyes too sharp.

As Nadia's gaze narrowed on Rathbone's figure below, Clara approached her, noting the troubled look on the young queen's face. "You're wary of him," Clara stated more than asked, her voice low but laced with understanding.

Nadia sighed, her fingers tightening on the balcony's edge. "He wraps his advice in wisdom, but I sense ulterior motives behind his words."

Clara leaned in closer. "The ways of court are new to you. Perhaps that is all that is troubling you?"

"But Aidan trusts him," Nadia countered, frustration lacing her tone. "He believes Rathbone is loyal to our cause."

Clara offered a sympathetic smile. "Aidan sees the strength in Rathbone's tactics. It is hard to argue against results."

"And yet," Nadia paused, searching Clara's eyes for some semblance of agreement, "something stirs beneath the surface... like whispers in a language I almost understand."

Later that evening, at a council meeting lit by flickering candlelight, Nadia challenged Rathbone openly. As he proposed tightening curfews to deter any lingering threats from Bellinor's sympathizers, Nadia interjected.

"Curfews would cage our citizens with fear," she argued, her voice carrying across the chamber. "Throughout history, restrictions like these have only bred resentment. In colonial America, curfews imposed by the British heightened tensions that eventually led to revolution. Similarly, during the Civil Rights Movement, curfews were tools of oppression that galvanized resistance rather than ensuring compliance."

The council chamber fell silent. Confused glances were exchanged across the polished table as advisors and captains tried to make sense of her references.

"America? Civil Rights?" Captain Grey muttered to Garin, who could only offer a slight shrug in response.

Councilor Rathbone's brow furrowed as he studied Nadia with newfound curiosity. "Your Majesty references realms unknown to us," he said with a careful precision. "Perhaps you might illuminate these... historical lessons in terms more familiar to Mirrathia?"

Nadia straightened, suddenly aware of the disconnect. "Where I was raised," she explained, "leaders learned that governing through fear undermines legitimacy. Restrictions like curfews create shadows for rebellion to grow. We must build trust with openness, not impose order through restriction."

Rathbone regarded her with an expression of mild surprise that didn't quite reach his eyes. "A noble sentiment indeed," he conceded smoothly. "Yet we must not be naive to the dangers that still lurk in our realm. Philosophy from other worlds may not apply to Mirrathia's unique circumstances."

Aidan spoke up then, siding with Rathbone. "My sister's perspective has merit," he acknowledged with a nod to Nadia, "but practicality demands caution. Precaution is necessary when shadows of Bellinor's influence remain."

"History repeats itself across all realms," Nadia countered, her gaze steady. "The Boston Massacre began with restrictive..." She stopped herself, noting the blank expressions around her. "What I mean is, when people feel trapped, they lash out. Let's not create the very rebellion we fear."

The room was thick with tension as brother and sister locked gazes; Nadia's filled with conviction and concern; Aidan's with earnest resolve. The moment stretched on as neither twin yielded ground.

Clara cleared her throat softly. "Perhaps there is wisdom in both approaches," she suggested. "Security without suffocation."

Talia, who had remained silent until now, watched the exchange with knowing eyes. She alone understood the full significance of Nadia's foreign references; evidence of a life lived in another world with its own painful lessons about power and governance.

Nadia stormed into her chambers, the heavy door slamming behind her with a satisfying thud that echoed her frustration. The council meeting had left her raw, her temples throbbing with the strain of maintaining composure while Rathbone's poisonous counsel seeped deeper into Aidan's mind.

She paced across the plush rug, its intricate patterns blurring beneath her agitated steps. The opulence of the room; tapestries of deep blue and emerald green depicting Mirrathia's landscapes, the ornate bed with its canopy of silken threads, the mahogany desk littered with scrolls... all of it suddenly felt suffocating rather than comforting.

Her gaze drifted to the corner of the chamber, where a large wooden mirror stood. She halted mid-stride, breath catching in her throat. The mirror, weathered oak frame with intricate carvings that had faded with time, was an exact duplicate of the one in her bedroom back in Mirrorlake. The same swirling patterns adorned its edges, the same slight chip marred the upper right corner, even the height matched perfectly.

Nadia approached it slowly, drawn by the uncanny familiarity. Her fingers trembled as they traced the familiar grooves of the frame, memory overlapping with present reality. This wasn't just any mirror, it was her mirror, the twin to the portal that had first brought her to Mirrathia.

"How did I not notice before?" she whispered, her reflection staring back with wide, questioning eyes.

She sank into an armchair facing the mirror, her mind reeling with implications. Through this looking glass, she could see not just herself, but the shadow of the life she had left behind; a bedroom with posters on the walls instead of tapestries, schoolbooks instead of royal decrees, and parents who understood her without the weight of prophecy between them.

"Is this what I am to be?" she murmured to her image. "A ruler in constant contention with my own brother?" Her words hung in the air, heavy with sorrow. "Arguing in council chambers over histories no one here understands?"

The familiar frame of the mirror seemed to offer a doorway not just between worlds, but between possible futures. In its reflection, she saw not a queen with a crown, but Nadia Calder, daughter of Sarah and Tom, student at Carrollton High, best friend to Jenny.

She leaned forward, pressing her palm against the cool glass surface. "I am their daughter," Nadia acknowledged, thinking of King Alaric and Queen Valora's blood in her veins. "But it was Sarah and Tom who nurtured me, taught me kindness and courage. Who listened when I spoke, even when I didn't make sense."

The mirror responded with silent understanding, its surface rippling slightly at her touch... not enough to open a portal, but enough to remind her that the connection remained. Home was just on the other side.

"It is not enough to wear a crown," she said, voice barely above a hush. "A ruler must also possess the wisdom to wield it well." Her green eyes hardened with resolve as she faced an unpalatable truth. "And perhaps wisdom means knowing when to step aside."

She rose, determination replacing doubt as she stared into the glass that had first shown her this world. The same mirror that could take her back.

"Perhaps Mirrathia would fare better with Aidan alone on its throne," she declared to her reflected self. "Without me to contradict him at every turn. Without arguments that weaken us both."

Her fingers traced the frame once more, following the familiar path of carved symbols that represented light and shadow—the very powers that flowed through her veins, powers that seemed increasingly at odds with her brother's.

"I must return home," she whispered, the decision crystallizing like ice in her heart. "For Aidan, for Mirrathia... for peace."

The mirror seemed to brighten at her words, as if agreeing with her choice, offering a glimpse of the bedroom in Mirrorlake that awaited her return; a simpler place where she understood the rules, where history made sense, where she belonged.

Under the veil of night, the gardens of Avaloria offered a serene backdrop for confessions and farewells. Moonlight filtered through the leaves, casting dappled shadows on the stone path where Nadia found Aidan waiting. He stood by the fountain, its gentle murmur a soft counterpoint to the turmoil brewing within them both.

Nadia approached, her steps hesitant but resolute. "Aidan," she began, her voice laced with a melancholy that mirrored the somber hues of evening.

He turned to her, his green eyes reflecting the sorrow of their shared predicament. "What weighs on your heart, sister?" Aidan's voice held a steadiness that belied his concern.

Nadia took a deep breath, finding courage in the openness of his gaze. "I need to return home," she confessed, her words floating like leaves upon the water's surface. "To Sarah and Tom... to the world that shaped me."

Aidan's brow furrowed, understanding dawning upon him. "You feel your path lies elsewhere," he surmised, not as a question but as an acknowledgment of her truth.

"Yes," Nadia affirmed. "Our parents gave us life, but it was my adoptive parents who gave me love and guidance." She clasped her hands together, seeking strength in their unity. "They deserve to know their daughter; not just as a reflection from another realm but as Nadia Calder, whole and true."

Aidan reached out, his hand resting upon her shoulder; a gesture of solidarity in a sea of uncertainty. "I always sensed your heart was torn between two worlds," he admitted softly.

Nadia looked up at him, gratitude shimmering in her eyes. "Will you stand with me in this decision?"

"Always," Aidan vowed, his own heart heavy yet supportive of her need to forge her own destiny.

Unseen by either twin, Rathbone hovered at the edge of shadow and light, his presence an uninvited whisper against the canvas of night. His lips curled into a sly smile as he drank in their exchange; a spider ensnared by the strands of fate they unwittingly wove.

With silent footsteps as soft as betrayal's embrace, Rathbone tiptoed away from the heartfelt scene unfolding before him.

Morning draped Avaloria in a cloak of tranquility, the city still stirring from slumber as Nadia made her way through the dew-kissed corridors of the palace. She had sought solace in the quiet, but the weight of her impending departure lingered with each step.

Her first visit was to Elan, whose laughter usually filled the halls. Today, his mirth was absent as he listened to Nadia's words. His grin faded, replaced by a solemn nod. "You have to follow your heart, Nadia. That's what makes you such a terrific friend."

Next was Mika, who greeted Nadia with her customary vivacious energy that quickly ebbed as she absorbed the news. "You're leaving us?" Mika's voice wavered. "But who will I share my wild plans with?"

Nadia smiled gently. "You'll craft even wilder ones," she assured.

Lina received the news with a sharp intake of breath, her quick reflexes momentarily stilled. "I can't say I'm not surprised," Lina admitted, her voice steady despite the sudden tightness in her chest.

Jorn, silent as ever, met Nadia's gaze and simply nodded, understanding without need for words.

With Lysara, it was different; her silver-blue eyes saw beyond Nadia's resolve to the conflict within. "Your journey is your own to weave," Lysara said. "And you weave it well."

Talia's response came with a gentle touch on Nadia's arm and a knowing look that conveyed volumes. "Paths diverge and converge in unexpected ways," Talia said, her voice tinged with foresight.

Later that afternoon, the council chamber brimmed with tension as Nadia stood before Captain Grey, Garin, and Councilor Rathbone.

Nadia addressed them all with composure born of conviction. "My time here has been... transformative," she began. "But I've realized my presence here isn't just about duty to a throne or realm; it's about being true to myself."

Captain Grey listened intently, his scarred visage betraying no emotion yet offering silent respect for her courage.

Garin's eyes softened as he nodded slowly, an unspoken understanding passing between them.

Councilor Rathbone watched from his place at the council table, his face a mask of benign interest while his mind whirred with unspoken calculations.

The room held its breath as Nadia continued. "I must return to my other home; to my parents, Sarah and Tom, to live the life they prepared me for."

The courtyard of the Palace of Light thrummed with the collective heartbeat of Mirrathia's people, gathered to hear their new queen speak. Nadia stood beside Aidan on the balcony, the morning sun casting a radiant glow around them.

"People of Mirrathia," Nadia's voice resonated with a mixture of strength and tenderness. "The light within me was ignited in this realm, but it was nurtured in another. I belong to both worlds, and I cannot abandon either."

Whispers fluttered through the crowd like startled sparrows, but Nadia's words hushed them as she continued.

"Aidan is your king, wise and just. Under his rule, Mirrathia will flourish." She turned to her brother, her eyes shimmering with unshed tears. "And I shall serve as the guardian of the portal, ensuring the safety of both our worlds."

Aidan's expression was a tapestry of pride and sorrow, knowing well the sacrifice woven into her words.

The assembly erupted in applause, accepting Nadia's decision with a respect that rippled through the air.

As preparations for her departure began, Nadia sought out Clara first. The healer's embrace was warm and soothing. "Your light is a rare gift," Clara said. "Guard it as fiercely as you guard the portal."

Next was Garin, whose eyes crinkled at the corners as he held Nadia at arm's length. "You've grown into more than I could have ever hoped for," he said gruffly. "Remember that courage comes in many forms."

Finally, Talia took Nadia's hands into her own. "The threads of fate are complex," she spoke with a serene smile. "Yours are interwoven with love and duty; strands not easily broken."

Later, as dusk painted the sky in shades of lavender and gold, Nadia pulled Aidan aside. They stood alone amidst the flurry of activity, their twin shadows stretching long on the ground.

"Aidan," she said with quiet urgency, "promise me you'll watch Rathbone closely."

Aidan met her gaze steadily. "I know your instincts are sharp, Nadia," he replied. "But Rathbone has proven himself valuable. I must trust those who served our parents."

Nadia searched his face for any sign of doubt and found none. She nodded slowly, trusting Aidan's judgment even as her own misgivings lingered.

"Promise me you'll be careful," she implored once more.

"I promise," Aidan assured her with a determined nod.

As night fell over Avaloria, Nadia took one last look at the city's illuminated spires, a beacon of hope she had helped reignite, and stepped towards her destiny as guardian between worlds.

The mirror's surface rippled like a pond disturbed by a gentle breeze as Nadia stepped through, the familiar confines of her bedroom greeting her. The room was just as she had left it, her books and posters a testament to the girl who had yearned for adventure and found it.

Nadia stumbled backward as the mirror's surface solidified behind her. The journey between realms always left her disoriented, but this time felt different—heavier somehow, as if the weight of her decision clung to her like a shroud.

"Nadia!" Jenny leaped up from where she'd been sitting on the bed, phone abandoned mid-scroll. "You're back already? It's only been like forty minutes!"

She rushed forward, relief evident in her wide eyes as she grabbed Nadia's shoulders. "I told your parents you were helping me with a SnapLife post in the backyard. They totally bought it."

Nadia blinked, struggling to process Jenny's words. Forty minutes? She'd spent months in Mirrathia; countless council meetings, battles, the coronation, the growing rift with Aidan...

"Are you okay? You look like you've aged a year in under an hour," Jenny said, her brow furrowing as she studied Nadia's face.

"What happened over there?"

Before Nadia could answer, a soft knock came at the door. "Girls? I brought you some cookies and lemonade," Sarah's voice called through the wood. "Jenny mentioned you were working on a school project?"

Jenny shot Nadia a pointed look that clearly said play along.

"Come in, Mom," Nadia called, quickly composing herself.

Sarah entered with a tray balanced on one hand, her smile as warm and familiar as the scent of the freshly baked cookies. "You two have been awfully quiet up here. Usually I can hear Jenny's laugh from the kitchen."

"Deep concentration mode, Mrs. Calder," Jenny explained cheerfully. "Nadia's been helping me with my history presentation. Super boring stuff."

Sarah set the tray down on the desk, brushing a strand of hair from Nadia's forehead with tender familiarity. "Well, don't work too hard. Your father's grilling burgers for dinner, Jenny, you're welcome to stay."

"Thanks, Mrs. Calder! I'd love to."

After Sarah left, closing the door behind her, Jenny turned to Nadia with wide eyes. "Okay, spill everything. What happened? Why are you back so soon? Did you defeat that creepy queen? Is your twin brother okay?"

Nadia sank onto her bed, the familiar comfort of her childhood mattress a stark contrast to the ornate royal chambers she'd left behind. "It's... complicated," she said, her voice barely above a whisper. "Time moves differently there. For me, it's been months."

Jenny's mouth fell open. "Months? As in... plural? While I've been sitting here scrolling through SnapLife for less than an hour?"

Nadia nodded, reaching for a cookie more out of habit than hunger. The sweetness tasted strange after Mirrathia's hearty fare. "We defeated Bellinor, but something's wrong with Aidan. There's this advisor, Rathbone... I think he's manipulating my brother. We fought about it, and I..." her voice caught, "...I left. I abandoned him."

Jenny sat beside her, their shoulders touching in silent support. "You came home."

"Yes," Nadia whispered, gaze drifting to the mirror. "Home."

In the days that followed, Nadia settled back into the rhythm of her life in Mirrorlake with surprising ease. Schoolwork, once a chore, now held a peculiar charm after months of royal decrees and battle strategies. The mundane banter of classmates, the scratch of pens on paper, even the stern looks from Mrs. Bell when eyes wandered during lectures; all were cherished as pieces of a life that felt both familiar and strange.

She walked the familiar streets with Jenny, their conversations punctuated by her friend's constant questions about Mirrathia, asked in hushed tones when no one else could hear. Yet even as she laughed at Jenny's quips about Mr. Kline's latest history assignment, a part of her remained attuned to the thrumming energy of that distant realm.

At home, Sarah and Tom noticed nothing amiss; to them, Nadia had never left. But sometimes she caught them watching her with curious expressions when she forgot to react to family jokes or mentioned events they hadn't experienced together. These moments were bridges between her two lives, reminders of the strange dual existence she now led.

Evenings were the hardest. As twilight descended and stars blinked into existence above, Nadia's thoughts soared across realms to Aidan. She wondered how he fared as king, whether he had discovered Rathbone's treachery. Her fingers would trace the cool surface of the mirror then, longing for answers that lay just beyond reach.

Nadia took solace in small things: the gentle brush of Sarah's hand as she tucked a strand of auburn hair behind Nadia's ear; Tom's proud chuckle when she bested him at chess; Jenny's conspiratorial wink across the classroom when they shared an inside joke about her "royal heritage." These moments anchored her, provided a bulwark against the call of duty that whispered through her dreams.

As autumn waned and leaves turned from green to fiery hues of orange and red, Nadia stood at her bedroom window, watching as they pirouetted to the ground in a final dance of defiance against winter's approach. She could feel Mirrathia pulsing in her veins; a persistent beat that harmonized with her heartbeat.

Turning from the window, Nadia caught sight of herself in the mirror. Her reflection seemed older somehow, wiser yet tinged with an indefinable yearning. She reached out, palm resting against the glass that separated two worlds, two lives, and felt its cool kiss against her skin.

In that moment, Nadia understood that while she might savor each day here in Mirrorlake, there would always be a part of her standing vigilant over Mirrathia. The journey ahead was hers alone to navigate, a path etched in light and shadow, and though it promised challenges untold, it was one she would walk with head held high.

With a deep breath, Nadia turned away from the mirror as Jenny burst into her room with her latest SnapLife post idea. The normalcy of it all was a balm to her restless spirit; a reminder that no matter where fate might lead her, this bond with her real world was unbreakable.

EPILOGUE: PORTALS AND PROMISES

Nine months had passed since she'd returned from Mirrathia, leaving Aidan to rule alone. The months she'd spent in the magical realm had translated to mere hours in Mirrorlake, allowing her to slip back into her life almost as if she'd never left.

But everything had changed the night Sarah walked into her bedroom just as Nadia was stepping back through the portal. She hadn't planned to go back... she just wanted to say hello to old friends. There had been no denying what her mother had seen with her own eyes. That night, with Jenny's blurry videos from Mirrathia as evidence, Nadia had told her parents everything. "We always knew you were special," Sarah had said, embracing her daughter. "We just didn't know how special." Since then, Nadia had lived her double life;

a normal teenager by day, guardian of the portal by night; though she hadn't returned to Mirrathia since that first trip back.

The familiar clatter of lockers punctuated the air as she made her way through a sea of peers, her gaze occasionally meeting those of classmates who offered fleeting smiles or nods.

In the classroom, Nadia's attention flitted between the drone of Mr. Kline's voice and the notes she scribbled, half-hearted attempts to capture the essence of the American Revolution. Her pen danced across the page, not with dates and names but with swirling patterns that echoed the enchanting landscapes of Mirrathia.

The final bell rang, signaling freedom and the promise of weekend revelry. Students spilled into the corridors, their voices a crescendo in anticipation of two days unburdened by academia.

"Hey, birthday girl!" Jenny sidled up to Nadia, a grin spreading across her face. "Can you believe you'll be sixteen tomorrow? Feels like just yesterday we were trying to talk your parents into giving you a Quinceañera!"

Nadia returned the smile, though it didn't quite reach her eyes. "I know, time flies. Are you coming over early to help set up?"

Jenny linked arms with her. "Wouldn't miss it for the world! We've got streamers, balloons, and I even made a playlist. Your SnapLife following has exploded since those 'special effects videos' we posted, but I made sure this party is just for your actual friends, not your internet fans."

They ambled towards their lockers amidst a flock of students discussing plans for Nadia's party. Excitement hung in the air like static, each conversation weaving a tapestry of anticipation.

"Yeah, I heard there's going to be an epic cake," one boy said as he passed by.

"I can't wait to see what Nadia's wearing," another girl chimed in from a group huddled by the water fountain.

Nadia felt a curious mix of elation and detachment. The festivities promised laughter and a night surrounded by friends; yet part of her longed for moonlit forests and whispered secrets on the wind.

As they reached their lockers, Jenny leaned in conspiratorially. "I snagged some fairy lights from my sister. Thought they'd add some magic to your backyard."

"That sounds perfect." Nadia's heart warmed at Jenny's thoughtfulness; her way of bridging two worlds.

The corridors began to empty as students trickled out towards various destinations. Nadia spun her combination lock, listening to the clicks that released her books from their daytime prison.

She closed her locker door to find Jenny beaming at her. "Ready for an unforgettable night?" Jenny asked, bouncing on the balls of her feet.

Nadia nodded, excitement finally sparking within her as she imagined friends gathered under a canopy of stars and twinkling lights; a night where she could be just Nadia Calder, if only for a little while.

Sunlight waned as Nadia and Jenny made their way through the familiar streets of their small town, the laughter and chatter of their classmates fading behind them. Houses with neatly trimmed lawns passed in a blur as they strolled side by side, a comfortable silence enveloping them.

"So, do you have a theme for tomorrow night?" Jenny asked, breaking the stillness between them.

Nadia shook her head, her long auburn hair catching the light of the dipping sun. "Just friends, fun, and food. That's all I really want."

Jenny's eyes sparkled with excitement. "Simple and sweet. I like it!"

They turned onto Nadia's street, the path they had trodden countless times before. As they approached Jenny's house, an impish grin spread across Nadia's face.

"Watch this," she said, glancing around to ensure no prying eyes lingered nearby.

Jenny watched, intrigued, as Nadia extended her hand toward a cluster of dandelions by the sidewalk. With a subtle flick of her wrist, the dandelions began to glow faintly, their white seed heads shimmering like tiny stars against the green grass.

"Whoa..." Jenny breathed out, her voice a mixture of awe and apprehension. "That's new."

Nadia closed her hand and the light snuffed out as quickly as it had appeared. She turned to Jenny with a triumphant smile. "Been practicing."

"That's incredible," Jenny admitted, though her brow creased with concern. "But you've got to be careful, Nadia. If someone saw that..."

"I know." Nadia nodded solemnly. "I just wanted to share it with you. I'll be careful."

Jenny's expression softened as she reached out to squeeze Nadia's arm reassuringly. "Just promise me you won't do any magical fireworks at the party tomorrow."

"No fireworks," Nadia promised with a laugh, "cross my heart."

Together they continued on to Jenny's front porch, their footsteps light and spirits high in anticipation of the celebrations to come.

Nadia waved goodbye to Jenny, her friend's door clicking shut behind her. She turned, a solitary figure now, her steps carrying her toward home.

Her house loomed ahead, the windows glowing with the warmth of inside lights. Nadia pushed open the front door, greeted by the familiar hum of life; her parents moving about in the kitchen, the faint murmur of the television from the living room. She exchanged pleasantries and made her way upstairs, her thoughts adrift on the morrow's festivities.

Her bedroom welcomed her with open arms, every object in its rightful place, save for one anomaly. There, near the weathered wooden mirror that served as her portal to another world, lay an unexpected sight; a gift wrapped in paper that bore the intricate symbols of Mirrathia.

Nadia approached, curiosity painting her features. The wrapping was done with meticulous care, the paper itself a work of art... silver filigree on a background of midnight blue. A ribbon of woven light held it together, shimmering with an ethereal quality that could only belong to Mirrathia.

With hands that trembled ever so slightly from excitement and wonder, Nadia undid the ribbon. The paper fell away to reveal a dress that seemed spun from moonlight itself. The fabric shimmered with a subtle iridescence, flowing like liquid silver when she lifted it into the air.

It was unmistakably from Aidan; only he would think to send such a breathtaking piece from across realms. A note accompanied it, his handwriting clear and precise:

"For your celebration in the world of your upbringing. May it remind you of the light you've brought to Mirrathia."

A smile touched Nadia's lips as she ran her fingers over the fabric, feeling a connection to Aidan and her other home in its weave.

The rest of her evening unfolded in usual fashion; a dinner filled with idle chatter about mundane matters, washing up and helping around as needed. But through it all, Nadia's mind often drifted back to the dress and its sender, a tangible reminder of worlds colliding and new beginnings.

In the solitude of dawn, Nadia stood before the old wooden mirror. She extended her palm, and with a fluid motion, conjured not just a simple orb but an intricate lattice of light that hovered in the air. Tiny motes of luminescence danced along its geometric patterns, each pulse synchronized with her heartbeat.

Beside her bed sat a collection of crystals - quartz, amethyst, and citrine - that she'd charged with her lightweaving. They emitted a gentle glow that brightened or dimmed with her emotions, serving as both nightlight and mood indicator. She'd discovered this technique by accident, finding that certain stones from this world could hold Mirrathia's magic, becoming reservoirs of power she could tap into when needed.

With careful concentration, Nadia drew the light from one crystal into her hands, then reshaped it into a miniature replica of Avaloria's palace. The tiny structure rotated above her palm, complete with spiraling towers and miniature windows that flickered with inner illumination. She added small figures moving through the courtyards - Aidan on his morning walk, Garin standing guard, Clara tending her garden.

These exercises had become her daily ritual; a way to maintain her connection to Mirrathia while honing her skills for whatever might come. She could now weave light into complex shapes and infuse objects with temporary enchantments, blending her magical heritage with the practical needs of her life in Mirrorlake. It was a silent affirmation of her role as guardian of the portal, a bridge between two worlds that depended on her vigilance and strength.

Yet even as she crafted these marvels with practiced ease, she pondered what it meant to lead a double life - to be a teenager with friends and homework on one side and a protector with magical powers on the other. The light palace collapsed back into formless energy as her concentration wavered with uncertainty.

A knock at the door jolted Nadia from her reverie. "Come in!"

Jenny burst into the room, her energy a stark contrast to the tranquility that had preceded her arrival. "Happy birthday!" she exclaimed, rushing over to engulf Nadia in an enthusiastic hug.

Nadia laughed, returning the embrace with equal fervor. "Thanks! I can't believe I'm sixteen."

Jenny bounced on the balls of her feet, eyes alight with excitement. "I've got so much planned for this weekend! But first," she glanced around the room with a conspiratorial grin, "let's talk about tonight's sleepover."

Nadia's heart warmed at Jenny's eagerness. The room filled with chatter about birthday plans and sleepover details, mundane yet precious, echoing off walls that held secrets of another realm entirely.

The room buzzed with the energy of two teenage girls plotting the night's escapades, their laughter mingling with the soft hum of anticipation. As they discussed who would bring which snacks and which movies were mandatory viewing, the atmosphere in Nadia's room shifted subtly. The old mirror, quiet sentinel of Nadia's dual existence, began to ripple as if a pebble had disturbed the surface of a still pond. A soft glow emanated from its depths, casting dancing lights upon the walls.

Jenny paused mid-sentence, her gaze drawn to the mirror. "Nadia, did you see..."

But Nadia was already on her feet, heart racing with a mix of alarm and recognition. She knew this phenomenon all too well; it heralded an arrival from Mirrathia. Her birthday, it seemed, would not be an ordinary one after all. Instinctively, she threw up a shield around herself and Jenny.

The rippling intensified until it was a maelstrom of light and shadow. Jenny stepped back, eyes wide with anticipation. Though she'd witnessed this before, the sight never ceased to amaze her. From within the swirling portal emerged a tall young man with short auburn hair and piercing green eyes that mirrored Nadia's own.

Aidan stepped into the room, his calm demeanor belying the extraordinary nature of his entrance. He took in the sight of Jenny, offering her a friendly nod, then turned his attention to Nadia. "Happy birthday," he said, a smile tugging at the corners of his mouth.

"Aidan!" Jenny exclaimed, rushing forward to greet him with the easy familiarity of old friends. "It's been ages! How's the whole ruling-a-kingdom thing going?"

The twins embraced, their connection a tangible force in the room. "I can't believe you're here," Nadia murmured, her voice muffled against Aidan's shoulder.

"Neither can I," Aidan admitted as he pulled back to look at her. His eyes shone with the same emerald light that danced in Nadia's, a mirror reflecting a shared past and an intertwined destiny.

The Calder living room brimmed with the quiet energy of an unexpected visit. Sarah and Tom sat on the floral-patterned couch, cups of tea cooling on the coffee table, while Aidan stood somewhat awkwardly in the center of the room. Nadia hovered by his side, her eyes darting between her brother and her adoptive parents.

"Mr. and Mrs. Calder," Aidan began, extending a hand that Tom shook firmly, "I'm Aidan, a friend from school." He mustered his most disarming smile. "It just so happens Nadia and I share a birthday."

Sarah's eyes twinkled with a mixture of amusement and affection as she cut him off gently. "Oh, Aidan," she said, "Nadia has already filled us in on everything."

Aidan's smile faltered for a fraction of a second before he regained his composure. "She did?"

"Yes," Tom chimed in, rising from the couch to clap Aidan on the shoulder in a fatherly manner. "Our Nadia doesn't keep secrets from us—not the important ones, anyway."

Nadia bit her lip, a rush of relief flooding through her at her parents' acceptance. She had been truthful with them upon her return from Mirrathia, revealing her heritage and the existence of another world beyond their own.

Sarah got up and wrapped an arm around Nadia. "We're just happy to finally meet you," she said to Aidan. "We've heard so much about your adventures together."

Aidan nodded, his posture relaxing as he realized the enchantments Talia had placed on Sarah and Tom had been lifted by honesty instead of magic. "Thank you for understanding; and for taking such good care of Nadia."

Tom glanced at Sarah before looking back at Aidan with a hint of pride in his eyes. "Nadia is our little miracle," he said warmly. "And it seems she's not our only one now."

Aidan met Tom's gaze with gratitude shimmering in his own eyes. It was clear to him that these kind-hearted people had provided Nadia with love and guidance when she needed it most.

Nadia felt a swell of emotions as she watched her two families merge into one harmonious unit; a reflection of her dual identity coming together under one roof. With Aidan's arrival into their lives, Sarah and Tom had gained another child just as miraculous as their first.

Laughter and the clinking of glasses filled the Calder home as Jenny and Nadia's parents celebrated Nadia and Aidan's sixteenth birthday over lunch. The dining room table, adorned with a blue and green tablecloth, bore a feast fit for royalty; though Aidan much preferred this warm, informal gathering to any regal banquet.

He marveled at the simplicity of it all; the chatter, the warmth, the unmistakable feeling of belonging. He watched Nadia flit around the room, her laughter mingling with the music that played softly in the background. Aidan found himself swept up in the normalcy of this world, a stark contrast to the courtly formalities of Mirrathia.

As the cake arrived, ablaze with candles, Nadia caught Aidan's eye and beckoned him over. Side by side, they blew out the candles together while everyone cheered. Tom captured the moment with a camera, preserving the memory of their shared wish whispered into the smoky aftermath.

Later that afternoon, Aidan sat beside Sarah on the living room couch as she leafed through an album filled with photos of Nadia growing up. Each image was a gateway into her life before Mirrathia; birthdays, school plays, family vacations; all moments he had missed but now felt a part of.

Nadia bounced into the room with news that drew everyone's attention. "I passed!" she exclaimed, waving a piece of paper triumphantly above her head. "I've got my driver's license!"

A round of applause erupted as Sarah rose to hug her daughter tightly. "We knew you could do it," she beamed.

Aidan clapped along with everyone else, his smile genuine and wide. The joy in Nadia's eyes was infectious, and he felt an immense pride in her accomplishment; a milestone in this world he was only beginning to understand.

"Queen in Mirrathia, driver in Mirrorlake," Jenny quipped. "Is there anything you can't conquer?"

Tom patted Nadia on the back with fatherly pride. "Just think of all the places you'll go now," he said, unaware of the double meaning his words carried.

The Calder living room transformed as streamers unfurled like rainbow serpents across the ceiling, their colors vivid against the soft white. Balloons bobbed in every corner, nodding their approval with each gust of air that brushed against them. Sarah and Tom moved with a practiced rhythm, hanging decorations and arranging furniture to create an open dance floor.

Nadia, Aidan, and Jenny tackled the food with gusto. Platters of bite-sized sandwiches, a battalion of cupcakes, and bowls of chips took their positions on the dining table, a savory mosaic ready for the impending feast. Aidan marveled at the pizza rolls, a delicacy he'd heard about from Lena but still found fascinating. He picked one up, carefully testing its temperature before popping it into his mouth.

"Still hot in the middle," Nadia warned too late, laughing as her brother's eyes widened in surprise.

"Your world's food continues to be both delicious and dangerous," Aidan remarked after he'd recovered. He glanced at Jenny's latest phone model with interest. "And your technology changes so quickly. That device is different from the last time I was here."

"Latest model," Jenny confirmed proudly. "Perfect for documenting royal visits from alternate dimensions."

Nadia slipped into the bathroom to change into Aidan's gift—the moonlight dress. The fabric felt alive against her skin, cool and warm at once, seeming to adjust to her body temperature perfectly. When she emerged, the dress caught the light and scattered it in prismatic patterns across the walls. Sarah gasped, Tom whistled appreciatively, and Jenny immediately pulled out her phone.

"This is definitely going on SnapLife," Jenny declared. "Your followers will lose their minds over these light effects!"

Aidan smiled, seeing his sister truly embody her dual heritage for the first time; a princess of Mirrathia dressed for a celebration in the human world.

As evening drew near, a buzz of excitement electrified the air.

The doorbell chimed its merry tune as guests began to arrive, each bearing gifts wrapped in glossy paper and wide smiles that mirrored Nadia's own.

Laughter cascaded through the rooms as classmates mingled, exchanging stories and jokes with ease. Aidan found himself amidst a group of Nadia's friends, sharing tales of his 'exchange student' experiences with animated gestures that drew chuckles and curious glances.

Music filled the house, a pulsing heartbeat that spurred even the most reluctant dancers into motion. The living room became an impromptu stage where friends showcased moves ranging from graceful to comically awkward. Jenny led a conga line, weaving through the rooms like a festive snake charmed by the beat.

Nadia beamed as she watched her worlds meld; the familiar faces from school now sharing laughs with Aidan, who had slipped into her life from another realm entirely. Her heart swelled with gratitude for this moment of unity; a blending of her two lives into one perfect evening.

The party thrived, a symphony of laughter and music, but Nadia's eyes often found Aidan. He seemed a shadow among the lights, a subtle crease in his brow, a glance cast towards the mirror standing sentinel in her room. When their eyes met, he offered a reassuring smile, but it never quite reached his eyes.

"Everything okay?" she mouthed across the room to him at one point.

"We'll talk later," he mouthed back, his smile straining against an unseen weight.

Nadia nodded and turned her attention back to her guests, but concern for Aidan nestled in her thoughts, refusing to be dislodged.

The time came for presents, and Nadia sat surrounded by colorful packages of all shapes and sizes. Her friends gathered around, eager to see her reactions. She unwrapped each one with care, thanking the giver with genuine warmth. Gadgets from classmates gleamed under the lights; books promised adventures within their pages.

Then Jenny stepped forward with a small box, wrapped in paper dotted with images of stars and moons; a nod to their countless nights spent stargazing. Nadia tore open the wrapping to reveal a delicate silver bracelet inside. Dangling from it was a charm: two hands clasped together.

"It's us," Jenny said, her voice tinged with emotion. "No matter where you go or what worlds you wander in... we're always together."

Nadia clasped Jenny in a tight hug, feeling the truth of those words resonate deep within her heart. The bracelet was more than metal and stone; it was a tangible reminder of an unbreakable bond. With careful fingers, Nadia fastened it around her wrist where it caught the light; a beacon of their enduring friendship.

The last of the guests filtered out the door, their voices trailing off into the night. The house quieted, save for the occasional clink of a spoon against a dish as Tom and Sarah tidied up in the kitchen. In the living room, Nadia, Aidan, and Jenny gathered on the couch, a small island in the aftermath of celebration.

"So," Nadia started, glancing between Aidan and Jenny. "What's going on? You've been looking like you're carrying the weight of two worlds on your shoulders all evening."

Aidan took a deep breath, his gaze fixed on the mirror that had served as their bridge between realms. "It's Mirrathia," he said, his voice low. "After Bellinor's defeat, we thought peace would last. But darkness has a way of creeping back when you least expect it."

Jenny leaned forward, her brows knitting together in concern. "What kind of darkness?"

"We're not sure yet," Aidan admitted. "But there have been... disturbances. Shadows where there should be light, whispers on the wind speaking of unrest. It's subtle, but it's there; something new and unknown."

Nadia felt a chill run down her spine despite the warmth of the room. "Is it Rathbone? I warned you about him."

Aidan's expression darkened. "You were right about him. He disappeared shortly after you left—vanished without a trace. But this feels different—older, deeper." He hesitated, then added, "Three nights ago, something extraordinary happened... a portal appeared. There have been rumors of a large flying beast in the forest."

Jenny leaned forward, eyes wide. "Wait... another world? There are more than just Mirrathia and Earth?"

"The ancient texts speak of many realms beyond our own," Aidan confirmed. "But now..." He looked directly at Nadia. "Now we know it's real. And whatever darkness threatens their world may threaten ours as well."

"I need your help, Nadia," Aidan continued, his green eyes meeting hers with an intensity that made her sit up straighter. "Whatever this is, it's beyond what we've faced before. I wouldn't ask if it wasn't serious."

Jenny reached out and squeezed Nadia's hand. "We're in this together," she said firmly.

Nadia drew strength from her friend's unwavering support and turned back to Aidan. "Tell me everything you know."

Nadia nodded slowly, the weight of her responsibility settling on her shoulders like a mantle. She had known from the moment she'd first stepped through the mirror that her life was no longer just her own.

"...and that's why we need you there, Nadia," Aidan finished, his plea hanging in the air between them.

"I understand," she said, her voice steady. "Mirrathia is as much a part of me as this world. I'll do what I must."

Jenny, who had been listening intently, offered a small, encouraging smile. "I'll take care of things here," she said. "I'll explain it to your parents. If anyone from school asks, you're with me on a study retreat for the weekend. They won't suspect a thing."

"Thank you," Nadia said, squeezing Jenny's hand in gratitude. She couldn't help but feel a pang of guilt for leaving her friend behind, but Jenny's resolve made it clear that she was just as committed to Mirrathia's safety as they were.

Aidan stood and offered his hand to Nadia. "Are you ready?"

She took a deep breath and placed her hand in his. "As ready as I'll ever be."

Together, they approached the mirror. The surface shimmered like water under moonlight, beckoning them to step through once more. Nadia cast a glance back at Jenny, who nodded firmly.

"Be safe," Jenny called after them.

With a shared look of determination, Nadia and Aidan stepped through the portal hand in hand, the cool rush of transition enveloping them as they left Nadia's bedroom; and their loyal friend; behind.

ABOUT THE AUTHOR

Amy N. Kaplan is an award-winning author who brings vivid worlds and memorable characters to life through her imaginative storytelling. Her love for fantasy began in childhood when she would create her own magical realms and adventures, a passion that continues to fuel her writing today.

When she isn't crafting tales of mirror worlds and twin heirs, Amy can be found playing tabletop games with her family, discussing her favorite fandoms, or hunting for treasures in antique shops. She lives in Texas with her husband and eldest spawn, while her other children have created their own adventures—two in Kentucky, one in Tennessee with her husband and two sons (Amy's beloved grandsons), and another in New Mexico with his partner.

Amy believes that stories have the power to transport readers to extraordinary places while helping them discover truths about themselves. Her hope is that readers of "Reflection's Reckoning" will be inspired to embrace their own unique gifts and find the courage to forge their own paths, just as Nadia and Aidan do in their journey through Mirrathia.

OTHER BOOKS BY AMY N KAPLAN

- Free Range Pigs: An Interactive Adventure Story About Three Little Pigs
- Free Range Bears: An Interactive Adventure Story About Three Bears
- Chronicles of Adventure: The Ultimate RPG Player's Companion
- Chronicles of Adventure: The Ultimate RPG Game Master's Companion
- Chronicles of Adventure: The Ultimate RPG Campaign Builder
- Chronicles of Adventure: The Ultimate RPG Campaign Creator Guidebook

WATCH FOR THESE EXCITING NEW TITLES

- Free Range Goats: An Interactive Adventure Story About Ten Little Goats
- Free Range Wolves: An Interactive Adventure Story About Three Wolves
- The Stone from the Dreamtime
- Nigel Needs A Home
- The Dragon Riders of Drakoria: The Mirror Kingdom - Book Two

9 781962 613255